THE ENIGMA

by

Jonas Saul

PUBLISHED BY:

Imagine Press Inc.
Ebook ISBN: 978-1-927404-24-9
Paperback ISBN: 978-1-998047-22-2
Hardcover ISBN: 978-1-998047-23-9

The Enigma
Copyright © 2013 by Jonas Saul

All rights reserved. No part of this publication may be reproduced, stored in a retrieval system, or transmitted in any form or by any means (electronic, mechanical, photocopying, recording, or otherwise) without the publisher's prior written permission.

This is a work of fiction. The characters, organizations, and events portrayed in this novel are either products of the author's imagination or are used fictitiously. References to real people, events, establishments, organizations, or locations are intended only to provide a sense of authenticity and are used fictitiously. Any resemblance to actual events, places, organizations, or persons, living or dead, is entirely coincidental.

Imagine Press Inc. does not have control over, or any responsibility for, any author or third-party websites referred to in or on this book.

The Sarah Roberts Series

Dark Visions (One)
The Warning (Two)
The Crypt (Three)
The Hostage (Four)
The Victim (Five)
The Enigma (Six)
The Vigilante (Seven)
The Rogue (Eight)
Killing Sarah (Nine)
The Antagonist (Ten)
The Redeemed (Eleven)
The Haunted (Twelve)
The Unlucky (Thirteen)
The Abandoned (Fourteen)
The Cartel (Fifteen)
Losing Sarah (Sixteen)
The Pact (Seventeen)
The Terror (Eighteen)
The Chase (Nineteen)
The Betrayal (Twenty)
Sarah's Return (Twenty-One)
The Hunt (Twenty-Two)
The Delivery (Twenty-Three)
The Trap (Twenty-Four)
The Ultimatum (Twenty-Five)
The Depraved (Twenty-Six)
The Condemned (Twenty-Seven)
Payback (Twenty-Eight)
The Unknown (Twenty-Nine)
Wrath (Thirty)
The Damned (Thirty-One)
The Game (Thirty-Two)

The Decoy (Thirty-Three)
The Disappearance (Thirty-Four)
The Whole Truth (Thirty-Five)
Alex (Thirty-Six)
Parkman (Thirty-Seven)
Darwin (Thirty-Eight)
Aaron (Thirty-Nine)
Remains To Be Seen (Forty)

The Jake Wood Novels

The Immortal Gene (Book One)
The Immortal Target (Book Two)

Standalone Novels

'Til Death Do Us Part
The Drowning
The Woman in the Woods
The Threat
The Specter
The Mafia Trilogy
A Murder in Time
Frequency of the Dead

Co-Authored Novels

Collision Course (Written with Gary Ponzo)
There Will Be Blood (Written with Rania Stone)
The Soulless (Written with Rania Stone)

Short Story Collections

Twisted Fate (Tales of Horror)

The Enigma

Twists of Fate (Tales of Hope)

Chapter 1

HE PEERED THROUGH THE downpour at the lights of the Las Vegas Police Department. The front of the building shone through the wet evening, every window emitting light, hope.

But there was no hope.

At least he didn't feel any. The picture he held gave him no hope. The darkness in his soul overwhelmed him as he stepped toward the bright building. How could he go through with it? It would change his life forever. It would put him in the spotlight, which he had worked tirelessly to avoid for the past two years. But if he didn't move forward, too many people would die.

His life as he knew it had ended when his daughter was killed.

Then the changes came. He took pictures. Things got better. But nothing would ever be the same without his little Penny. Nothing. Ever.

In front of the police station, the American flag hung limp and soaked on its pole, giving him reason to pause and reflect on his lovely country. The violence, the weapons, the shootings, and what it all meant for future generations, what it meant for him in the coming days.

After a moment, he wiped his eyes and walked to the shelter of the front doors, where he slipped inside and dripped on the tile floor. His stomach twisted in a sick dread at what he had to do.

Why me?

He shook off his overcoat, brushed back his dark brown mane, and wiped his face. A uniformed female officer sat behind a glass partition, like one found at any ticket booth at a bus or train station. People waited at various spots throughout the room. Two men were reading, and two stared into space. One older man, who didn't look like he had showered in months, sprawled out on two chairs, biting his fingernails.

Russell Anderson moved farther into the room until he was close enough to the little booth that the female officer looked up from whatever she was doing. She didn't smile or nod. Not impolite, just all business.

"Can I help you?" she asked.

Her teeth were so white and perfect that he couldn't help but stare at her mouth as she spoke. It helped to avoid eye contact.

He cleared his throat. "Detective Collins, please."

"I'll see if he's in."

She typed on her computer, paused, then typed again.

"Looks like he's in a meeting." She turned to him. "Can I have another officer come speak with you? Or do you want to leave Detective Collins a message?" She blew out of the corner of her mouth at a loose strand of hair. The bun at the top of her head had lost its shape. He considered taking out his camera to take her picture, but it didn't seem right.

The cop looked him in the eyes. She didn't gawk at the four-inch scar that ran from his temple to his jaw on the right side of his face.

"No message. I'll wait." Russell turned and started for the chairs.

"Excuse me," the woman said behind him.

He stopped but didn't turn around.

"Sir?" the woman said again.

He pivoted on his heels in slow motion until he was facing her.

"Your name?" she asked.

This was the part he had dreaded. Letting the cops know his identity was not the plan. Russell had taken six pictures over the last two years and mailed them to Collins. His identity would complicate things and make it too difficult to live in Vegas. He abhorred the spotlight. But it was a crime if he offered a fake name and was found out. He didn't come here to be arrested.

If he were arrested, people would die.

"I need a name," the woman tried again. "Then I'll send a message to Detective Collins that you're waiting for him."

"Very well. Do you have a pen and paper?"

He stepped back up to the window.

The officer rummaged in her desk and produced a pen and paper a moment later.

"Is your name too hard to spell or something?" she asked.

As he took the proffered pen and paper, he caught her quick glance at the scar.

Just like everyone else.

He wrote his name down.

Russell Anderson.

"I don't want it spoken out loud," Russell said as he capped the pen and handed it back under the glass partition. "Others may hear it. Please respect my wishes."

The woman reared her head back on an angle, hair loosening from the bun and framing her pretty face. "Ohhh, I get it. Right. Okay." She leaned closer to the glass partition and whispered, "Then I'll *type* my message to Collins. I won't say it out loud."

"Thank you," Russell said and stepped away from the window. She could make fun of him if she wanted, but this was his life. The more the police knew about him, the worse his life would become. He would probably have to leave Las Vegas anyway when everything was over in the coming days. It had been his home for six years. Soon it would be a memory—a painful memory. He was being called to Toronto, but he didn't know why yet.

He sat in the waiting area, rubbed his hands together, and kept an eye on the others lounging in their chairs. Maybe he should've called first. Perhaps he could've set up an appointment with Collins. Met him in a Starbucks. Told him what he needed to say to him there. That could've worked. But Collins would have been too suspicious because his mission over the previous two years had been to put Russell behind bars for murder. He had been unsuccessful in that endeavor, however relentless he had proven to be.

Outside, the rain insisted on cleansing the city. On the one night Las Vegas got blasted with rain in the middle of August, which was rare, he had to walk to the police station.

Smart. Real smart.

He looked down at his hands. After a moment, he glanced up at the clock on the wall. Time was running out. He didn't want anyone else dying because of him. He'd lost his daughter and still had the scars to prove how hard he fought for her. But it was his fault, and no one could take that away from him. He would own it until the day he died, which he hoped was soon. He wasn't suicidal, only wishing God would see it in his plan to take him early.

Please forgive me. Then take me home ...

"Anderson," someone shouted in the cavernous room, making Russell bounce in his chair. It echoed a few times before he could say anything.

"Is there a Russ—"

"Here!" Russell shouted loud enough to drown out the cop's voice as he faced the man, his arm raised.

They locked eyes. He could tell the cop was perturbed at being cut off, but Russell didn't care. It was his name, and to have it shouted in a room full of strangers was disrespectful and downright rude. Russell had to remain anonymous, and he would cut the cop off again if he tried to speak his name out loud.

The cop dropped his arms to his side and jerked his head toward a corridor. "Come on."

Russell followed the cop through a winding maze of hallways and endless doors. The man was dressed like Russell would expect a detective to dress; the nice collar shirt, tie and dress pants. He had a folder in his hand, but Russell had no idea what that could be since no one knew he was coming. Maybe the police brought one into every meeting with new visitors so they could start a file on them.

The man opened a door marked number four and gestured for Russell to go inside.

"Can I get you a water or a coffee?" the man asked.

Russell shook his head and walked to the far wall of the small room, taking it all in as the cop shut the door, leaving Russell alone. The table, the two chairs, the window on the side. A little speaker-like thing on the wooden table had a wire that exited its base and dropped below the table, where it connected to a box plugged into the wall.

They're going to record this.

He could never let that happen. They would commit him for psychiatric assessment if who he truly was became public knowledge.

Russell walked around the table twice, studying the walls, the mirror, and finally, the microphone. He unplugged the unit from the wall and settled down a little, breathing better.

After what felt like ten minutes, he tried the door. It was locked.

What the hell?

He tried it again, this time putting his shoulder into it. The door wouldn't budge. He wasn't a prisoner. He had come of his own free will. What the hell were they thinking?

He backed away from the door and faced the mirror. No doubt they were watching him. But for what? They had no idea why he was there. No idea what was coming. Only he did. It was a favor to them that he had come there on a rainy evening.

Or rather, a favor to Sarah Roberts. But he didn't want to think of that yet. Not until Collins arrived.

He closed his eyes and rubbed his temples as he leaned

against the back wall. Breathing rhythmically, he forced his heartbeat to slow below a hundred beats a minute. It wouldn't serve anyone to hyperventilate or pass out. He arrived with a purpose, and he intended to fulfill it.

The door opened. A man stepped in, followed by a pretty woman.

Do the Vegas cops only hire pretty women?

They held Dixie cups, probably filled with coffee. This man held the same file folder unless the cops all used the exact same brand and size.

"Please, have a seat," the male said.

Russell stayed against the wall.

The man closed the door and moved to stand beside the woman.

"I'm Detective Bruce Collins, and this is my partner, Detective Mara Munro. I understand you're …" he paused to twist the file in his hand and read something. "Russell Anderson?" He looked back up to meet Russell's eyes, an expectant look on his face. "Did I get that right?"

Russell nodded.

The detectives exchanged a glance, then looked back at Russell.

"Well, you got me," Collins said. "You walk in here, ask for me by name, and now that you have my attention, you don't say a word. Is there a joke somewhere, or are you just wasting our time?" He glanced away like a thought struck him. Then he met Russell's eyes again. "I'm the investigating officer on the murder of your daughter, Penny Anderson."

Russell waited. He had no idea where to start. No matter what he said, they would deem him insane. They wouldn't believe him. This had been a waste of time. But there was nothing else he could do. He had to try.

He closed his eyes and took a deep breath while rubbing the bridge of his nose.

Something smacked loudly in the room. Russell opened his eyes. Collins had tossed the folder onto the table.

"That's you," he said.

Russell shivered under his coat. The air conditioners were relentless in Vegas during August. It felt like none of them had stopped as the sun dropped and the rain started. His clothes were damp, and his skin coated in moisture, which felt like a thin layer of ice now that he was victim to the cooler inside air.

"What's me?" Russell asked.

"That folder. Everything we've got on you."

"Surprise, surprise."

The detectives exchanged another glance.

What's with them looking at each other?

"What do you mean by surprise?" Collins asked.

Russell adjusted his coat, fixed his hair as it had fallen down over his forehead with the dampness, and moved to take a chair.

They waited as he sat and got comfortable. He interlaced his fingers together on the table and looked from Collins to Munro, then back at the table.

"What I have to say cannot be recorded."

He watched as Munro followed the cord on the floor to the wall and then back to Russell.

"It's unplugged," she said.

"What about behind that mirror?" Russell asked, unlocking his fingers to point.

"There's no one there," Collins said. "You came to see

us. You're not a person of interest in any crime at this time. At least none that we're aware of." He looked at his partner again.

"Don't do that," Russell said.

"Excuse me?" Collins gasped.

"You two keep exchanging glances like two teenagers in a high school math class. You'd think the two of you would be comfortable in your relationship as partners by now."

"Before I arrest you for something or kick your ass back out into the rain, do you mind telling us why you came here tonight? Was it just to waste our time?"

Collins was irritated. Russell hadn't planned for that, but he couldn't, nor wouldn't, hold back. The world was shit. People were shit. The only thing stopping him from a bullet in the mouth was he couldn't off himself. Therefore, he had no reason to bullshit, take any, or let disrespect go unanswered.

Fuck them if they didn't like it.

Russell opened the folder and scanned the first page. Police reports on the murder of his little girl. For a brief moment, he fought the urge to slam the folder shut and storm out of the building. How could they know it was him so fast? His name alone? His facial scar? He wondered if they had facial recognition cameras installed in the new police building. That must have been the reason for the delay in meeting with Collins. They wanted to know who they were talking to and record the conversation if anything had to do with the case that many thought didn't get properly handled —the case of the murder of Penny Anderson, Russell's only child, her mother deceased during Penny's birth.

He flipped the page, and the eyes of the dead woman

who stole his baby stared back at him from when she was alive and well—or maybe not well.

Was she ever sane?

He closed the file. He couldn't look at the sick fuck who had stolen his daughter and used a knife on his face and his daughter's body. He hadn't come for that, and he wouldn't discuss his life or the death of his child with strangers anymore. That chapter of his life was closed, as was his heart.

The detectives had been patient as he looked in the folder. Munro had eased a chair back and sat while Collins chose to stand, but now he leaned against the two-way mirror, arms crossed.

"You gonna tell us why you came here today?" Collins asked.

"I have a message for you."

"Oh, yeah? From who?"

"Me."

Collins uncrossed his arms and pushed off the wall. He was a good cop, Russell decided. He was ready, alert, and smart. This would give Sarah Roberts a chance. Collins's partner, Munro, seemed like a good backup.

"I am your mystery man."

Collins frowned. "Mystery man? I'm not following."

"You get mail here. Typewritten addressed envelopes. Inside, you find a picture that is time-stamped and dated. You will also find a typed note explaining the picture. From the newspapers, I can tell you put it all together and solve the crime." Russell looked down at his hands. "All except that one with the suicidal banker." He looked back up at Collins, his eyes rimmed in tears. "How's that? Huh? Cleaning that man's brains off the hotel room wall? Oh, I would guess detectives don't do the cleaning, do they?"

Russell wiped his face and composed himself. His outburst didn't seem to affect either cop.

"How do you know about the pictures?" Collins asked.

Munro appeared confused. She looked back and forth between Russell's and Collins's faces.

"What's this about pictures and suicidal bankers?" Munro asked under her breath.

"Before your time," Collins said.

"How long have you two been partners?" Russell asked.

"Six months," Munro answered.

"Then two of the photos were not before your time, including the banker. He died tragically five months ago. The hospital photo I mailed in a few weeks ago has not been dealt with, as far as I know."

Collins shot his partner a look. "I'll talk to you about it later." Then he stepped to the table and glared down at Russell. "How do you know about all this?"

"A moment ago," Russell said. "I assessed you and decided you were smart, street-smart. I might have to change that assessment."

Collins slapped the table with his hands. "Stop fucking around, Anderson, and tell us what the hell you're here to tell us."

Russell tried to collect himself. He ground his teeth together. "Say my name again, and I will walk out that door and leave you two to clean up the mess." He swallowed hard and twisted his neck to loosen the muscles. "I am so sick of this life, so please, say my name again. I want to leave." He spoke through his teeth. "Try me. Just this once."

Collins visibly calmed down and stepped back. Something in his eyes told Russell he was ready to listen.

"Fair enough," Collins said. "You have the floor. Tell us what it is you've come to tell us."

Russell waited a moment, then decided to explain everything.

"I am the man who sends you the pictures. We needed to get acquainted. It is important that you know it's been me who has helped your career because it'll add weight and credibility to what I am about to tell you."

Collins cleared his throat and snuck a glance at Munro. Russell wasn't sure if Collins would engage his ego and get mad at the career comment. He could order Russell out of the police station or stay humble and listen to what Russell had to say. If he listened, he was the right man. If not, Russell would ask to see someone else.

The tension between the two detectives felt like the moment before a boxing match started. The gloves were on, the sweat already running, but not a single punch had been thrown yet.

"Okay, you know more about the letters than anyone in this department but me and the sheriff. Why don't you start by telling me ..." He stopped and gestured at his partner when she glared at him—evidently, he hadn't been keeping her in the loop. "I mean, *us*, how you know when to take the pictures and how you know all the other information you add in the envelopes."

Russell shrugged. "There's no easy answer for that."

Collins clapped his hands and then spread them wide. "That's great. No easy answer. Terrific. Well, I don't believe you. How do I know whether you're involved in some way with each crime and missing kid that we've solved because of those pictures?" He stopped talking to pull out his cell phone.

"What're you doing?"

"I'm calling the sheriff in here. He's gonna want to meet the man who has mailed us anonymous letters and pictures. Don't ya think?"

"Set your phone down, Collins," Russell said in a steely voice. "If you don't, I walk, and Jake might not make it."

Collins stopped, his thumb hovering over the buttons. For a moment, he stood frozen, staring down at his phone. Without looking up, he asked, "Jake who?"

"Put your phone away," Russell said. "This meeting is for the three of us. You can tell the others whatever you want when I leave, but for now, it's just us."

Collins waited for a heartbeat, then slowly put his phone away and glared at Russell.

"There have been two abductions," Russell started. "One robbery, one hospital betting racket, and two suicides that I've sent to you. How could I be involved with suicides, one of which you let happen? On the kidnapping, the news said the abductors gave up when you found the compound in the desert. I haven't heard about the hospital one yet, but that was pretty recent—"

"We're working on it," Collins cut in.

"Are you clear now that it's me sending you the photos?"

"Yes, but I still don't know why or how, although I would agree it's you. Is this visit because of another photo, another crime? A missing person? A suicide?"

Detective Munro pushed back from the desk and got up from her chair. She was clearly lost, and it was obvious that her partner hadn't been candid with her.

"I'll be waiting at my desk since this has nothing to do with me." She turned to Collins and glared at him. "You've made that abundantly clear." Then she stomped out the door and slammed it closed.

"Ouch," Russell said.

"She'll be okay. That's my problem. Now tell me, what has happened that brought you here today?"

"It's not what's happened this time. It's what's going to happen."

"Huh? You're always in the right place at the right time with your camera. Your photos have helped us forward those cases to a conclusion. Now you're saying that something is *going* to happen? That means no pictures, right? I mean, you can't take a picture of the future, right?"

Collins seemed to be coming undone. What had changed? Was this personal for him? Or was he concerned that Russell's message was about brother Jake?

Russell reached into his jacket pocket and pulled a plastic bag out. Inside the bag, the picture was still dry. He unzipped the bag and retrieved the photo.

"This is a pic of a woman. You may have heard of her in the news over the last few years. Her name is Sarah Roberts."

Collins took the photo and stared at it. "Seems to ring a bell. Didn't she break up an FLDS compound a while back?" He snapped his fingers. "That's right. She's been in Europe or up in Canada for some time." He met Russell's eyes. "I read about her a few months back."

"She'll be in Vegas tonight, or she already is."

"Has she committed a crime?"

Russell shook his head. "She's in danger."

"How can I help with that? There's a lot of people in danger at any given moment."

Russell waved at Collins. "Listen to me closely. Within the next thirty-six to forty-eight hours, people will be murdered on the streets of Vegas. Sarah has arrived to try to stop it, but it will only worsen. I understand that the text she sends starts everything in motion. There will be no stopping the murder, possibly even hers …" he trailed off to gather his thoughts. He didn't want to ramble. He felt spent, exhausted.

"How do you know all this?"

"I confirmed my identity with you at the beginning of this meeting to bypass that trivial question. I will not and cannot discuss where I get my information. All you need to know is that if Sarah sends that text, people will die as early as tonight or tomorrow. I will try to help her, but I'm not sure I can. Frankly, I'm not sure how."

"Why come to me? You know cops don't work that way. I have to have a crime to investigate. I can't work with things that *might* happen. What exactly do you want me to do with this information?" Collins stepped back, crossed his arms, and leaned against the wall by the mirror.

"I understand your position even better than you do," Russell said as images of his daughter flashed into his mind and what little help he received from the police when he needed them. "I brought this to you because it involves you."

"Oh really? How so?"

"When you meet Sarah, she will ask you to do something for her. I need you to do it. Even though you won't want to."

"Are you serious?" Collins slapped his leg as if Russell had just said the best joke in a long time. "Okay, if that's all I have to do—"

"Take this seriously. If you don't, Jake will be killed, and Lana will be left without a father for her children. Do you understand me?"

Collins stopped horsing around and stood rock still.

"How do you know my brother's and his wife's names?" Collins asked. "Are you threatening my family?"

Russell figured those names would help his plea and get Collins on board. Before this meeting, he had no idea that Jake and Lana were related to Collins.

"Jake is your brother?" Russell asked.

Collins slapped the table again. "How do you know his name?" he shouted.

Anger surfaced in Russell. "I have no idea," he shouted back. "It's the same with the photos. Do you think I know why I take the pictures I do? Or what they mean when I'm taking them? Come on, you're not a fool. Think about it. The only reason I'm still in Vegas is that I believe my natural father lives here."

"I'll ask you again. Are you threatening my family?"

"I'm leaving." Russell got up and moved for the door. "This has been a waste of time."

Collins blocked his way. Russell didn't stop until they were nose to nose.

"Do what Sarah Roberts asks of you," Russell said. "Or *you* hurt your family, not me. If you refuse to listen to Sarah, she will die. Of this, I'm certain. Then the newspapers will pick up the story that Sarah Roberts is dead. If they don't, I will tell them that I brought this to the Las Vegas Metropolitan Police Department, to Detective Bruce Collins and his partner, Detective Mara Munro, and they fumbled the case. Now, step aside. I'm fucking well leaving. I've committed no crime and came here of my own volition. Try to stop me, and Jake dies. Try to stop me, and the photos stop coming. Are we clear?"

Collins panted like he'd been running. Russell was close enough to smell the sandwich Collins had for dinner and the coffee he'd washed it down with. He held his breath to keep his own stomach contents where they were.

Collins waited for another heartbeat and then stepped aside and opened the door.

"What if you're wrong?" Collins asked, his voice low and controlled.

"What if I'm right?" Russell answered.

He slipped through the door and started down the hall. Then he stopped and turned around.

"Collins?"

The detective stood in the doorframe of room four but didn't say anything.

"I wasn't here. Forget my name. Don't say it out loud or whisper it to a colleague. I'm anonymous. If I don't get anonymity, I'm through. You will never see another photo from me again." He pointed a finger at Collins. "I chose you because I was told you were the cop who would handle the information I mail with the photos in a manner befitting an officer of the law. So far, you've done a stellar job, except for that banker." Russell paused for a moment. "Keep the picture of Sarah. I left it on the table. Do what she says when you meet her. That's all you have to do."

"Why not mail it in like all the other photos?"

"Sense of urgency. Sarah's coming. You will meet her very soon. Then it all starts." He extended his arm out and pulled back the damp sleeve to look at his watch. "Two hours."

"What starts?" Collins asked.

Russell turned around and continued down the corridor.

"Good luck, Collins," he said over his shoulder. "That woman might have killed my three-year-old little girl." His voice broke, and he had to swallow the emotional lump in his throat. "But the man who drove her to do it hasn't paid for his crimes yet. We will all be meeting in due time."

Russell turned the corner and walked out of the police station. His hands were shaking, his stomach a mess. He walked on, hoping he didn't collapse in the police parking lot.

The rain had subsided. The night had warmed again.

If only it were a harbinger of things to come.

Chapter 2

Sarah Roberts broke open a bag of trail mix while waiting for the rain to stop. She leaned against the bridge's concrete wall and stared at the underside of the Mojave Freeway as she chewed. The bridge offered ample shelter from the rain.

She had notes. She had a plan. All she had to do was drive into Vegas, find a random man with a cell phone, and get him to text a number Vivian had supplied. The note was specific. It had to be a random male, and the text had to read, *Don't do it—keep the money*, which meant nothing to Sarah.

It was Vegas, after all. Maybe a gambler was about to bet too high, and this text saved his bank account or house. Or even better, his marriage.

Sarah had received one other note. It offered instructions for her to go to a building on the outskirts of Vegas where she would stop a man from being tortured. She had no idea who the victim was or why she had to stop the torture. None of the reasons mattered. When her dead sister asked her to do anything, she did it. The messages were too important. They always had been.

The subtle din of the rain hitting the pavement subsided. She checked her cell phone. It was still early enough to get a good night's sleep. She would ride into Vegas, probably stay near the strip, find her random man with a cell phone, send the text, and then check into a hotel. Saving a guy from torture wasn't supposed to happen until after midnight. Maybe Vivian would say more later.

She packed her trail mix away, stowed the novel she had planned to read if the rain had continued, and slipped her helmet over her head.

It had been a long few months, and fatigue seemed to be the norm. She needed a break.

If only Vegas could be that break, she thought.

She whipped her leg over the seat and straddled the new bike, a present from her parents, after they sold their old house and moved to Santa Rosa, California. She'd had no idea that riding a bike could feel so liberating.

There were regrets, though. One of them was Parkman. She missed him. They had worked so closely together in the early days, but now he was starting his own private investigation service. The police force he worked for had denied his last leave of absence, but he'd gone anyway. Staying on in Toronto to help her had cost him his job and his pension. Yet he seemed happier than ever.

Maybe one day, his services would help her, and they would work together again. At least she knew where he was and could reach him at a moment's notice.

She swung the bike around, drove out from under the bridge, and turned onto the ramp. The road was wet, but the rain had stopped. The lights of the Gold Strike Hotel lit up the corner of the road as she rode up the ramp to the freeway. She would be in Vegas soon with just over twenty miles to go.

Maybe a nice meal before she sent the text. Maybe a hot bath in a hotel room. She deserved it. It was the time to relax.

Take it easy on me, Sis. I need a break.

Something told her this wasn't going to be easy. Send a random text. Stop a torture session.

What the fuck does that even mean?

She still didn't know where the torture was supposed to happen.

She opened up the bike and hit seventy-five miles an hour quickly. The faster she got to Vegas and completed these tasks, the sooner she could relax and have that hot bath. With bubbles. And wine. And twelve hours of sleep in one bed. Uninterrupted.

I wish.

She lowered her head and drove the bike harder along the wet freeway, the vibration of the powerful machine between her legs energizing her for the coming days.

Knowing Vivian, Vegas wasn't going to be easy.

Chapter 3

KRISTI RAINE SLIPPED OUT of her track pants and T-shirt and grabbed her black dress, which she used to wear when she first hooked up with Tyrone. She touched the fabric, and rubbed her fingers over it, remembering how he looked at her when she wore it. Lately, he was drunk, stoned, or angry when he looked at her. Their relationship hadn't been the same since her dog was killed.

She wanted out of Las Vegas. The tourists didn't see the shit people like her and Tyrone lived with every day. This city was a money magnet, and with money came every sort of criminal element.

She put the dress on but would need Tyrone to zip it up. Her arm still hurt from their big fight two days ago. She had to watch her mouth. She knew that, but sometimes he said things that hurt. He laughed at her because she was sad her dog had died. He had been a good German shepherd. Trained well, too. She had no idea how he got out of the trailer after she went to work. Tyrone said when he got home, the front door was wide open. He almost called the cops thinking they'd been broken into.

Rocky was found out by the road, his head nearly removed by a passing car.

It was so unlike Rocky. But he was dead, and there was nothing Kristi could do about that.

Barefoot, she walked through the trailer and found Tyrone in front of the TV. A rerun of some sitcom played on such a low volume she had no idea how he could hear it. Maybe he only watched it for the chicks. On-screen, two different bimbos in tight V-neck tops argued about which one was going to date some guy.

Kristi looked around the kitchen. It was overrun by empty beer cans and discarded pizza boxes. The small two-bedroom trailer reeked of stale air and vomit. For a man in debt up to his gonads, he sure spent a lot of money on takeout. Tyrone's friend had lent them the trailer when they got kicked out of their apartment for not paying the rent. They were supposed to be gone last month. By Monday, Tyrone's buddy would come to evict them. Then they would be royally screwed. No place to stay, no money, and mounting debt.

She had begged Tyrone to leave Vegas with her. They could start fresh somewhere else, just the two of them. But he was always knocking her idea down. His friends lived here. His life was in Vegas. After her dog died, she just wanted to stop living in the trailer that reminded her of him. At least by Monday, they'd be gone.

It was as if Tyrone lived oblivious to the world around him. The hole he dug might bury him if he didn't do something about it soon.

She had been the one who came up with the idea for the scam. So far, it looked like it was going to work perfectly. She had to leave within the hour, and everything would work out. They would be okay again.

"Can you help zip me up?" she asked, trying not to interrupt his show.

"Zip it up your own fuckin' self."

He was in one of his moods again.

What a great night to be going out.

"Tyrone, I'm doing this for you. The least you can do is help me get dressed."

He mimicked the sound of a baby. "Oh, widdle widdle baby girl can't get dressed by her widdle self?" He smacked his beer can down on the table by his chair and turned to her. "Zip what?" he snapped.

She turned slightly and showed him her back. With a hard tug, the zipper raced up and caught her skin at the base of her neck.

"Hey!" she yelled. "Take it easy. That fucking hurts."

"Well, then, next time, do it yourself. I'm not your fucking servant."

She turned back around. He was already drinking from his beer can again. She got down on her knees beside his chair. Something wet and mushy squished under her legs.

What the hell ...

"Tyrone?" she said in her soft, mothering voice.

He stared straight ahead, his eyes locked on the TV, ignoring her.

"Tyrone?" she said louder.

"What?"

"If this works out, we're getting a cool ten grand tonight.

That'll help, right?"

The contempt in his eyes when he turned to her was a far cry from how he used to look at her when she wore this dress.

"You are such a stupid bitch," he growled. "You think ten grand will fix us up? I owe Maxwell Ramsey almost fifty grand, and my payment is late. Do you know what he does to people who are late? You should because you're with me. We together." He pointed at her and then at himself. "Maxwell hurts people who owe him money and the people they love, too. That's you, baby." He raised his voice, obviously drunk. "The love of my life."

She wanted to cry. Tyrone's heart was so big. She'd seen it before. He loved her and had shown it to her by taking her out for dinner. They'd been together for over four months, but after losing his job and getting kicked out of the apartment, he changed.

He had stopped being a runner for Big John two months ago, and that was when he stopped making money, at least the kind of money he could gamble with. Becoming a professional gambler just wasn't in the cards for Tyrone. Borrowing fifty-thousand dollars from Maxwell Ramsey had been a huge mistake, but they went way back. Big John had Tyrone make routine deliveries. But now Tyrone was put out on the porch, as he put it. Used up. Over. Finished.

When they fought a few days earlier, she had cried over his comment that since they couldn't afford food anymore, it was a good thing Rocky was dead because they sure as hell wouldn't be buying dog food.

But that was the past. She understood Tyrone. He was a man like any other, and he had held jobs and gone through lots of money in his life. He'd done it once, he could do it again. He just needed a break. And when he got it, Kristi wanted to be there for him.

They could start living again if they could pay the fifty grand back.

"Maybe after I get the ten grand tonight, I could milk the idiot for more." She waited to see if Tyrone wanted to snap at her again. It was okay with her if he needed to because it allowed him room to air his anger. Once all the rage was out, sex was better. When he was drunk or stoned or angry, sex was horrible or too rough. Or nonexistent. "Can you get a small time extension from Maxwell? Maybe I can get all the money within a couple of weeks—"

He turned toward her, color coming to his face. "Why do I put up with you? Are you really that stupid? Or wait, are you trying to be a *fucking* comedian?"

She lowered her head and stared at the carpet in front of her bare knees.

"Ask him for an extension," he shouted. "He's not my fucking bank or a high school teacher waiting for my essay. No, he's a small-time gangster-loan-shark motherfucker." Tyrone jumped out of his chair and threw his beer can across the room. It smacked against the empty fish tank propped up on concrete blocks.

He stomped into the kitchen and grabbed another beer from the fridge. She knew to be quiet and let him vent on his own. Speaking to him when he was angry only added bruises to her already growing collection.

"Maxwell Ramsey has a reputation to keep." The beer can popped as he opened it. After a long chug, he continued. "I owe him fifty grand like yesterday, bitch. I don't come up with the money, you know who be losing a finger or a toe, or worse? Me, that's who." He lowered his voice and walked back to the chair. "It's better I stay here in the trailer. He doesn't know where I am. You go get that ten grand from your little pet asshole. Bring it back here. Maybe we take off. Start a new life."

She lifted her head and wiped her hope-filled eyes.

"Really?" she asked.

"Sure, baby. You go get the money and come back here. But don't tell nobody where you going, woman. Come back after midnight when all these fucking nosy neighbors are asleep. Sneak in the back way. We'll take the money and leave before the sun rises."

She was afraid to get her hopes up too far. "Are you … serious? Would you really go away with me? Just like we talked about?"

"Course I'm serious. Just don't fuck this up. Make sure you get that money." He took a long pull from the beer. "What, you think Ramsey is all-seeing, all-knowing? How the hell he gonna find me in Canada?"

She clapped her hands together and chirped. He gave her a sidelong glance and frowned. She didn't care. When she was happy, this was how she showed it.

"Let's do it," Kristi said. "Let's leave Las Vegas behind. We can do it. Ten grand should take us a long way."

He set his beer can down and turned to her, his hands out, palms up.

"Take my hands."

She did, tentatively.

"It's okay. I'm not going to hurt you."

His hands tightened on her fingers, softly grinding the

knuckles together.

"Look me in the eye and tell me what you're going to say to this idiot you're meeting tonight. What's his name again?"

"Jake Collins."

"What you gonna say? What you gonna tell him?"

Kristi shrugged. "It's easy. He thinks I'm pregnant. We drank too much at that party and ended up sleeping in the same room. I joked around in the morning, saying he had been so good in bed. I wanted to tease him and make him feel like he pleased me. I was just joking. I thought nothing of it. I mean, he flirted with me so much the night before. And my girlfriend thought it was hilarious."

"Yeah, I know all that shit," Tyrone said. "What you gonna say?"

His patience was wearing thin.

"I got his business card. You remember I found it when we were packing to come to live here. Anyway, I called and told him I had gotten pregnant. I asked for money for an abortion and to go away, to leave him alone—hush money. He agreed to bring me ten grand in cash. There's nothing really to say to him, Tyrone. He's flying in from Phoenix right now. Once we meet at the New York, New York bar Cowboy Ugly on the second floor, I get the money and leave. His wife and kid never need to know. I don't think he wants small talk. There'll be nothing to say."

"Oh, man, do I have to tell you everything? Yo momma ever teach you about men?"

"I guess so. What are you saying—"

"You tell that dirtbag, once you already have the money in your purse, that he got you pregnant and that you need another forty grand, or you will keep the baby, and he'll pay child support for the next eighteen years. And on top of that, you will have to tell his wife, too. He needs to think that his life is over without forty more grand."

"But I'm not pregnant."

Tyrone's hands squeezed tighter. "I fucking well know that, but he doesn't. Just listen."

Her knuckles ground together, making it hard to concentrate on his words. If she tried to pull away, he would hurt her worse. Better to just wait until he let go.

"He will agree because he's married," Tyrone said. "And he doesn't want his wife to know about his little mistake in Vegas. Doesn't he own some big company or something?"

"You're hurting me," Kristi whispered. She had to say something. Just when she thought his hands were too tight, they got tighter.

"Focus, bitch. Don't worry about your fingers. See, that's what I'm talking about." He tightened his jaw and breathed through clenched teeth. "You gotta learn to focus on what's important. You fuck this up with that asshole, and you fuck up our whole life. A little pain in the knuckles ain't hurt nobody. You get it?"

She nodded, afraid to open her mouth in case she gasped or cried out. Tears edged past her eyelids.

"You wanna go away with me, don't you?" he asked.

She nodded vigorously.

"Good, then fucking listen to what I have to say."

The pressure on her numb fingers magically relented, and she breathed easier as he stopped squeezing and only held them. The blood circulating again tingled under the skin of all eight captive fingers.

"What company he own?" Tyrone asked.

"Something to do with metal or steel."

"And he was in Vegas five months ago at some convention at the Venetian?"

"That's where I met him." She nodded. "The party was in one of those huge rooms upstairs. His company had blocked off an entire floor."

"Right, so what I'm saying is, this guy has the money to pay out large, and you got the assets. You gotta do this before you show a baby bump."

She clucked her tongue. "But I won't show a baby bump because I'm not pregnant."

He tossed her hands away. "Get out of my sight before I call an ambulance."

The dress was tight, but she could stand up without ripping it and stare down at him. "An ambulance?"

"Yeah, because I'm gonna hurt da bitch you don't go get me my money."

Kristi headed for the bedroom and her one suitcase. She needed her makeup kit to finish getting ready. Maybe after she was all done up, Tyrone would smile when he looked at her again.

She flexed her hands and winced at the pain in her fingers.

Why does he always have to show how strong he is?

She was ready in twenty minutes. She hoped Tyrone still had the money for the cab and hadn't spent it on beer. She was already going to be late.

She peeked outside through the small bedroom window. The rain had stopped. She slipped on her black heels, checked herself in the mirror one more time, grabbed her small purse, and walked back into the living room.

Tyrone was asleep in the chair, the beer can resting at a forty-five-degree angle in his hand on the armrest.

"Hey, Ty, where's the money for the cab?"

She nudged him. He grunted in response.

"Tyrone, the money?"

Nothing. He was out. A beer coma.

She scanned the dirty kitchen and spied his wallet by the keys on the counter. Stepping over garbage, a pizza box, and three crumpled beer cans, she made it to the counter by the fridge.

After a quick look over her shoulder to ensure he was still sleeping, she opened his wallet. Inside she found three hundred-dollar bills. Another furtive glance back at him, then she grabbed all three. In a few hours, she would return with ten grand. Three hundred was nothing to ten grand. Besides, he would probably still be asleep when she got back.

All she needed was cab fare, but the extra could buy her a nice dinner or maybe new perfume.

Maybe she could drop some money in a slot machine. If she hit it big, they could pay off Ramsey and live the high life somewhere else, away from the lure of fast cash and organized petty crimes.

She slipped the money into her purse and opened the door to leave.

"Kristi?" Tyrone said behind her.

She froze. Her stomach dropped to her ankles. If he saw her take the three hundred from his wallet, maybe she would need that ambulance after all.

"Good luck," he slurred out of his drunken stupor.

She closed and locked the door, making sure the knob clicked tight.

She didn't breathe normally until she was six trailers away.

Chapter 4

Detective Collins watched Russell until he rounded the corner at the end of the hallway. He waited for a few moments and then walked back into interrogation room four, grabbed Russell's police file and the picture of Sarah Roberts. Before leaving, he plugged the recorder back into the wall and exited the room.

Three steps down the hall, he entered the viewing room adjacent to room four.

Munro was reviewing the recording of their meeting with Russell.

"I knew that's why you left," Collins said.

She looked up at him. "I'm still pissed. How come this is the first I've heard about these pictures and letters?"

Collins peered through the two-way glass in room four. "The sheriff wanted to keep this particular anonymous tip anonymous."

"Even from me, your partner?"

She didn't sound angry as much as disappointed.

"Even from you."

She grunted.

"The letters are always addressed to me," Collins said. "After I opened the first one, followed up the lead, and made an arrest, I took the letter to the sheriff."

"What made you take it to him?" Munro asked. "Why was this one special?"

He turned from the window and met her gaze. "Because it foretold the future."

"How's that? A photograph? That doesn't make sense. If he took a photo yesterday and then a crime happened, how could the photo be about the future?"

"The photo doesn't tell the future; the message does."

"More confusing."

"Let me explain." He sat in one of the chairs. "The first picture I got in the mail was of a little kid in the arcade at Excalibur. You know the one."

She nodded.

"There was a man in the photo standing behind the kid. It was a full facial of the perp. The note said the man was stalking the boy and would kidnap him. Once he had the boy, he would drive him to an abandoned compound twenty miles out in the Mojave Desert, where the boy would die seven days after arriving at the compound."

"Wow. Bold statements. Any of it true?"

"All true." Then he realized he wasn't being clear enough. "I mean, it was true about the kidnapping. The compound, too. But the boy didn't die because we got the letter and the photo. From the photo, I could identify John Simmons, who was known to the San Diego Police Department. Two priors."

"That's it?"

Collins shook his head. "There were directions to the compound in Russell's note. I drove out there with my old partner before your time and found the compound. Inside, we located the boy, starving. He'd already been there three days. Then we set up a stakeout and waited for Simmons to show. He did later that night. The arrest was effortless. The boy lived. His parents are forever grateful."

"Why three days? Why didn't you go as soon as you got the letter?"

"USPS."

"Huh?"

"The letter was sent the day the boy was taken. It took a couple of days to get to us. By the time I read it, looked into the image of Simmons, and matched the photo of the boy with any new missing persons cases, I thought we had to take that tip seriously. It was twenty-four hours from receiving the letter on my desk until we entered the compound, which was some old hippie bunker."

"Yet you weren't convinced of the letter sender's veracity? Why not?"

"Never believed in fortune tellers." He looked down at his polished shoes. "I was beyond ecstatic that we had rescued the boy, but always wondered if the photo was sent by an accomplice who got cold feet."

"That's why you're a detective now."

"Then more letters came."

"Are you a believer?" Munro asked.

"I have no choice. But it's Russell Anderson who's been sending me the letters. I just don't know anymore. I just don't know."

Munro scrunched her eyebrows. "You don't know anymore? What does that mean? Who is this guy?"

"You haven't read his file."

It wasn't a question, but Munro shook her head.

"His daughter, Penny Anderson, was murdered two years ago. She was only three years old. It was a tragic case."

"Tell me about it."

"Penny's mother died at birth. Russell has priors. Apparently, he decided to do right by his new daughter. No more gang banging. He gets a job, finds an apartment, and takes care of his daughter. At three years old, Penny comes down with a nasty flu. She's hospitalized. No one knew about the crazy aunt. Russell slept by his daughter's bed day and night, waiting for her to come out of the coma."

"How do you know all this?" Munro asked.

"It was my case. I mean, this is a kid we're talking about —I needed to make sure nothing got missed."

"What else happened?"

Someone knocked on the door. Other officers needed the room.

Collins and Munro headed upstairs to an empty conference room, and Collins got them both a coffee. Once seated, he opened Russell's file.

"It's all in here if you ever want to go through it."

"Give me the abridged version."

"Russell leaves his daughter's room for the cafeteria. It's seven in the morning. Hospital staff are changing shifts. Everyone's tired and sluggish. When Russell gets back to the room, Penny's gone. Naturally, he panics. At the nurse's station, he learns that no one has transferred Penny anywhere. As far as they're concerned, she's supposed to be in her room. After alerting hospital security of a possible kidnapping, Russell runs through the hospital and ends up outside at the front. He claims he saw a woman with a bundle in her arms running into the bush a few blocks away. He gives chase. When he catches up with her, his daughter Penny is already bleeding from knife wounds. When he grabs the woman, she slashes Russell in the face and arm. After that, she drops the blade, tosses Penny's body aside, and runs down the street, hollering like Lucifer's inside her."

"Wow. Insane and sad." She sipped her coffee.

Collins took the opportunity to sip his, too. "I know. It gets worse. Russell sees that Penny has succumbed to her injuries, sets her down gently, grabs the knife, and takes off after the woman. Soon he collapses from blood loss, and you can assume the rest."

"Yeah, he would've been charged with the murder of his own child unless someone saw this woman. I mean, you've got a murder weapon with his prints on it. You'd need motive and a few other details, but once you have a body, a weapon, and prints on the weapon, not to mention he was probably covered in blood from what investigators could assume were self-inflicted wounds …"

Collins shook his head because his mouth was full of coffee again.

After swallowing, he said, "He was definitely a person of interest, but the murderer became an unidentified subject, an UNSUB. We had only one witness to corroborate Russell's story. No charges were laid at first. Then, six months later, the woman shows up and confesses. She lays out her statement identical to what Russell had said happened. This woman, Penny's aunt, didn't want Russell raising her sister's daughter. That's the end."

"What happened to the aunt?"

"She's dead."

"Dead?"

Collins nodded and then drank the rest of his coffee down. He set the empty cup on the table and stared at it.

"The aunt died in custody. You probably heard about it. Injected with enough heroin to flatline an NFL team. No one knows how she got the drugs inside the cell."

"She was searched when she got booked?"

"Of course," he said. "Oh yeah. Cavity search. Everything."

"Cameras?"

"We checked everything. All we have now is a dead child, a confession, and a dead murderer. The file was officially closed, and the small task force that had been assembled was dismantled before you transferred to our city." He waved a finger in the air. "There was always something about Russell that bothered me, though. I have no idea what it is, but there's something."

"You think he did it? Maybe paid the woman off to confess and then killed her? That theory wouldn't be a stretch if he did kill Penny."

"No, he's not that smart. Besides, she really was the aunt from Hell. Had a history of being committed for psychological evaluation. I just don't like how it all went down. It's crazy that Russell just walks in here and asks for me. I was the lead investigator on his case. I'm the guy who was trying to put him behind bars for the rest of his life. Why send me those photos and letters?" He said this last part almost to himself.

"What was that shit about your brother?" Munro asked. "Sounds to me like this dude is psychic or something, whether you want to believe it or not."

Collins pushed away from the table and got to his feet. He walked to the door and stopped. "If he was psychic, why not save his daughter?" He looked at Munro. "That's why I don't believe in that shit. People are always psychic when it's convenient, not when it really counts."

"What about that picture of Sarah Roberts? We both know she's done some crazy shit. I hear she's an automatic writer. You may not believe in that, but I do. I know Sarah has spent time in hospitals herself after stopping the very perps we're trying to nab. To some, she's a hero. To others, a fake."

"What's that got to do with me?"

Munro got out of her chair and joined him at the door. "Russell sends you photos and notes on where to find a kid who was kidnapped from the Excalibur Hotel. You solve that case and a few others. Now he shows up and tells you to listen to Sarah Roberts to save your brother. I'd say the best advice is for you to listen to Russell and do what Sarah says whether or not you believe in any of it." She opened the door. "Forget Russell's history. Irrelevant here. Play the cards he's dealing with. So far, you're both winning."

She started down the hallway.

"Hey, where're you going?"

Over her shoulder, she said, "I'm giving you the privacy of the conference room to call your brother. You need to find out why he will be in trouble later." She stopped at the end of the hall before turning the corner. "If Russell Anderson is correct, Jake will pay the ultimate price if you don't play

Russell's game. The end result will be on your head and only your head. Russell will look like the good guy because he warned you, which seems to be something he's good at." She disappeared behind the corner.

Collins stepped back into the room and pulled out his cell phone. He was so busy with his job that he never talked to Jake anymore. The last time they spoke was when Jake flew into Vegas for a work-related conference at the Venetian. That had to be at least five months ago.

Lana answered after two rings.

"Hi, Lana, how's everything?"

"Bruce? Is that you?"

"Good job. Considering how often I call, I'm surprised you recognized my voice."

"I thought you'd call."

What the fuck?

"Turning a little psychic on us, now?" Bruce asked.

"Hold on a sec," Lana said.

She pulled the phone away from her ear, followed by a clunk when she set the phone down. In the background, he heard her talking to Michael, his brother's seven-year-old.

There was a gnawing in his stomach. An ominous feeling that something was coming, and it wasn't good. Even calling his brother in Phoenix felt wrong. He had to know what was happening but didn't want to buy what Russell Anderson was selling.

A moment later, she returned to the phone.

"Now, where were we?" Lana asked.

"I was just saying how we don't get together often enough."

"I know. You'll have to come out for the weekend before

the summer's over. They give you time off at that strenuous job, don't they?"

"Of course. We'll do that. I'll put in for a few days and come down. Listen, could you put Jake on?"

"Funny."

He frowned at the odd response. "Funny? How do you mean?"

"He's with you, isn't he?"

The gnawing grew to serious chewing. His legs instantly loaded up on adrenaline, and he had to take a seat.

"Why would he be with me?"

"He flew into Vegas this afternoon. Said he had a business meeting tonight and that he would be having dinner with you. Maybe I heard him wrong. Maybe he said he would call you and try to steal you away for dinner."

He had to get to Russell again. He had to talk to him to find out what he knew. What was going on? Could Russell orchestrate such an elaborate scheme to get back at the one cop who worked tirelessly to put him behind bars?

"That must be it, Lana. Jake has probably tried to get in touch with me. I've been tied up at the station all day and night. I'll check my messages."

"When you see him, tell him to call me. Michael's going to bed soon, and Jake said he'd call."

"He didn't call yet?"

"No. I've tried a couple of times myself, but it goes straight to voicemail."

"Okay, I'll tell him—"

"Oh shit, Bruce, I gotta go. Michael's knocked his glass of milk over."

"Okay, okay, go."

"Bye."

"Wait—what hotel did he say he was staying at?"

The phone clicked in his ear.

"Shit."

Jake was in town. He hadn't called Bruce. And Lana couldn't get a hold of him. What the hell does Russell Anderson know?

Collins dialed his own voicemail. After listening to all the messages and skipping the ones he'd saved, there was nothing from his brother.

He left the conference room. He needed to find Munro. Their shift ended soon, but he wouldn't be going home. They needed to do a search on Russell Anderson and find out everything they've got on him that's current. And he had to find his brother and make sure he was okay.

Then he had to find Sarah Roberts and see if she was even in Vegas. Whatever she needed to tell him, he wanted to hear it.

For now, he was willing to believe his brother's life hung in the balance. Too many things were adding up too fast.

If anything happened to Jake, he would arrest Russell Anderson for it unless evidence said otherwise. He had video from interrogation room four that would show Russell uttering death threats to the family member of a detective with the Las Vegas Police Department.

The same detective who nearly arrested Russell for murder two years ago.

Maybe this had nothing to do with clairvoyance after all and everything to do with revenge.

Sweet, simple, cold, calculating revenge.

Bruce dialed his brother's cell number and listened as it

rang until voicemail kicked in.

Chapter 5

THE BRIGHT NEON LIGHTS of the big city flashed on and off as Sarah maneuvered along the strip, weaving her bike around taxi cabs and stretch Hummers. The sidewalks were jammed with people.

She passed under a walkway bridge between the New York, New York Hotel and the MGM Grand Casino, which was lit up a beautiful green.

Traffic was tight, the going slow. Caesars Palace was coming up on the left after The Bellagio. On the right, she saw Planet Hollywood Casino, the Paris Hotel, and Bally's. It was quickly overwhelming for someone who didn't gamble —at least not with cash. There were too many lights, the allure of fast money, and the high life.

She turned off the strip onto Flamingo Road and found a parking spot to squeeze her bike into. She'd find her guy, send the text, get back on the bike, and locate a hotel off the strip to check in for the night.

The helmet stuck to her hair when she tried to pull it off.

Getting used to having long hair again seemed to be a lifelong chore. Only six years ago, she would pull out that hair, one small clump at a time. It had felt good then. Now, it just pissed her off when her hair was pulled.

She set the helmet on the back of the bike, brushed off her jacket, and swung her hair off her shoulders. The sky was already clearing, the clouds that had let go on the city earlier moving away. Stars shone down on the lights of Vegas but were lost to the artificial charm of the gambling mecca.

She took a second to ensure no one was paying her attention. After checking her gun had a full magazine, she stuffed it in the back of her jeans.

She was ready.

"Vegas, here I come."

She walked half a block to the strip, turned left, and joined the foot traffic. The past few years had given her a complex. Even though she'd never been to Las Vegas nor had plans to stay, she always expected someone lurking in the shadows. Some would call that paranoia. Sarah called it survival.

She walked up an escalator at the corner and used the walkway above to cross the busy road below. On the other side, Bally's tower rose high, with water performing unique tricks in the fountains.

She jumped and raised her arms in defense at a loud whooshing sound. As fast as her arms came up, she dropped them out of embarrassment.

Across the street at Bellagio, water shot out of the fountain at least a hundred feet high. As she watched, the water danced to the melodic sounds of Celine Dion.

Even from the other side of the road, Sarah stood

transfixed by the free show. People lined the railing by the water where strategically placed speakers belted out the music.

Then she saw him.

A man with a scar on the side of his face.

She kept her eyes locked on him. He stood at the base of the escalator, twenty feet away, watching her.

They locked eyes for several seconds before she shrugged and raised her hands, palms open in a what's-up gesture.

He didn't move. Only kept staring.

So she started toward him.

"Two simple tasks," she whispered, shaking her head. "That's all I'm supposed to perform. Vivian, this your doing?"

The man broke eye contact, brushed his wavy hair out of his face, and then spun on his heels and jumped on the escalator going up.

Sarah broke into a run. He was halfway up when she hit the bottom and started her ascent.

"Excuse me, excuse me," she said as she edged past people.

She caught a quick glimpse of the scarred man turning left at the top toward the Bellagio. Seconds later, she turned left and looked along the concrete walkway above the strip.

He stood by the doors to the Bellagio, holding one open. They stared at each while she collected her breath. Then he said something, but it was drowned out. She moved forward a few steps.

"What?" she called.

Passing strangers looked at her.

"Don't send the text," the man shouted.

The text? How the fuck does he know about that?

She started walking. "Who are you?" she asked. "Come talk to me."

More people stared; others turned to look at her. Mostly, everyone just kept walking, minding their own business. A vagrant down on his luck sat in a corner, his hand out. She grabbed a handful of change from her pocket as she passed him and dropped it in his upturned baseball cap.

The scarred man at the door moved backward into the building.

"Hey, wait," she yelled and started running again.

He disappeared inside, the door shutting. There was enough light inside the building for her to see him through the glass doors as he ran in about twenty feet and turned right, where he disappeared behind a wall.

She hit the doors and jumped past two women for whom a man had opened the door. At the corner, she turned right. The man with the scar was gone. Another door led out onto yet another walkway.

She went to those doors and stepped outside, but the man had disappeared. The walkway to Caesars Palace had at least a dozen people on it, but he was gone.

"Sarah?"

It wasn't immediately obvious who had spoken her name as she looked at the people walking by her.

"Sarah?" the voice called louder.

It was coming from the edge of the walkway. She moved over cautiously and peered over the edge, her hand near her weapon. The man with the scar on the street below stared up at her.

"I didn't catch your name," she shouted down. "How do you know mine?"

"Don't send the text," he shouted back.

"What's it to you?" she called down.

From where she stood, it looked like he was crying. He rubbed his eyes and twisted his fingers over them several times.

"Just, please, don't," he said.

Mystery Man walked away.

Behind her, a small stairwell led down to the sidewalk. Should she give chase?

She decided it wasn't worth it. Unless he were willing to come up and explain to her why she was not supposed to send the text, then she would do it. No one on earth would stop her from doing what Vivian asked her to do unless that person had a very good reason. One they could *prove* to her was a good reason. Vivian had done right by her for over five years. Sarah wasn't going to deny her sister because a stranger told her to.

It bothered her that someone she had never seen before could know about the text. It was one thing to know she was in town and recognize her face. But it was quite another to know what she was supposed to do. That had always been private between Vivian and her. It was virtually impossible that anyone else would know.

She headed through the Bellagio, used the walkway to cross back to Bally's area, and descended the escalator to the street. Vegas was big, the lights bright. She didn't want to get too far from her bike and end up lost.

She had memorized the phone number she was supposed to text. Why couldn't she just use her own phone to text it?

That was the thing with Vivian. It was implied that Sarah would follow the message to the letter and do her best never to deviate.

So she had to locate a random man and get him to text the message.

She walked along the strip, passing Bally's and then the Paris Hotel, waiting for the right face and guy to use.

On her right, near the edge of the street, she passed men and women holding little cards for people to grab. As far as she could tell, it was prostitution advertising. They'd slap the cards in their palm to make a noise and then jam them out in front of people.

It started to piss her off. Every time she passed one of them, their hands thrust out fast, almost making her slap them or knock the person's hand away.

Discarded pamphlets and garbage littered the edge of the street. People walked by, drunk, boisterous, and partying. Others drank in the street. She passed two girls who couldn't be a day over eighteen, sipping from a straw that was inside the top of a blue balloon with Paris Hotel and Casino printed on it.

She needed a drink. Red wine and a bath. No more delays. It was time to find a random guy, send the text, and then find a hotel.

A man walking alone came toward her. She slowed and sized him up. Something about him seemed furtive like he was on full alert. He checked behind him but then kept coming toward her.

She stopped by a fenced-off construction area and waited for him to get closer. The area she picked sat between two streetlights, and it was down a little from the main casino's front doors. This was one of the darker areas on the strip, which would work perfectly.

When the man was a few feet away, Sarah checked to see if the scarred man was back and then stepped in front of her random guy.

"Hey," she said.

He stopped fast and even stepped back a foot.

"What?" he asked.

He tried to look strong and tough, but Sarah saw fear in his eyes.

"I've got a problem," Sarah said.

"Yeah? What's that?"

Now he was playing the tough-guy act. It was so easy to see through.

"I need to use your cell phone."

"What? No way."

"Look, I have to send a text to someone. It's important. I know this is random, and it seems crazy to you, but can you cut a girl a break? I just need to send a text, and then I'm gone."

"Use your own phone," he said and started to walk around her.

She grabbed his arm and pulled him back. He almost lost his balance and had to take several steps to right himself.

"Hey, what the fuck?" he shouted.

People looked at them, probably assuming they were just another couple who had lost too much money at the tables and were arguing about it.

"Send the text for me, please," she said with a smile. She dipped her head low and let her hair fall off her shoulders and into her face.

He didn't fall for the female persuasion. Instead, he backed away until he bumped into the fence, looking even more afraid.

"Are you with Maxwell Ramsey?" he asked.

"Who's that?" Sarah asked.

"Maxwell Ramsey? You never heard of him?"

She shook her head. "New in town." She waited a heartbeat. "The text?" This was taking too long.

"Fuck you," he said and pushed off the fence.

As he moved past her, she grabbed his arm and shoved him hard. He teetered back and bounced onto the fence again. Then she moved in close.

"You're not playing nice," she said. "I've picked you as my random guy. That means you're going to send the text. There's no other option. It's a simple fucking text. What's the big deal? Do a random act of kindness here."

People moved by behind them, oblivious to the scuffle. They probably thought the young couple was getting frisky before heading to their room.

"Get off me," he protested.

He tried to force her off, but she rooted her feet in and angled her hundred-twenty-five-pound frame into him, holding him against the fence.

She leaned in close to his face. "Are you going to help me, or do I have to force you? I would rather this go easy, but I can do hard."

"Fuck you," he said jand pushed away from the fence again.

She whipped out her weapon as she lowered her center of gravity and came up into his gut with her shoulder. He doubled over and fell back into the fence.

She brought the gun up and under his chin, protecting it from prying eyes with her body.

"Holy shit," he said, swallowed hard, then breathed in and out fast. "Okay, okay, I'm sorry. I'll send the text. Just don't shoot me."

"Keep your voice down. Whisper."

He nodded vigorously.

"Now, I'm going to put the gun away. You're going to play nice, right?"

He nodded so hard that his hair flew around like he was on a roller coaster.

She slipped the weapon back into her pants.

"Now, pull your phone out, slow and easy."

He reached into his jacket pocket and eased out a cell phone.

"Set up a text to this number." She gave him the number from memory. He did as he was told.

"What do you want me to say?" he asked.

"Type in, 'don't do it—keep the money.'"

He did.

"Now hit send."

They watched as the message was sent, and then the phone showed the word *delivered* below it.

"Perfect. Delete the number from your messages."

She watched as he did that and then moved back.

"That's it?" he asked, breathing easier now.

"That's it. Wasn't so bad, now was it?"

"You're fucking crazy. Loco bitch."

He stepped away from the fence.

"Hey, watch your mouth, or I'll wash it out with a little metal."

She didn't feel right having to deal with her random stranger this way. She had asked politely. If he had just given her a free text with his phone, he would've received a smile and even a sexy thank you. Instead, he wanted to be a dick and even forced her to pull out her weapon.

What's wrong with people today?

This wasn't her style. But once she'd chosen him as her random guy, she had to stick to it. He had to be the one. It had to be his phone. That's the way it was with Vivian's messages. Any deviation and people could get hurt. Even killed.

She deviated before and paid the price. She would never deviate again. When Vivian said she had to pick a random man and get him to use his cell phone to text the message to that number, that's exactly what she did, and screw the consequences. She would never see that guy again. He can go on for the rest of his life and wonder who that strange girl with the gun was who made him send a text that night in Vegas.

The guy walked away from her, looking over his shoulder periodically. Thirty feet later, he glanced back once more, then hailed a cab.

Sarah exhaled audibly. It was done. The text had been sent. Now, for the hotel, the bathtub, and then stop a torture session.

Wonderful.

She headed back toward her bike. How was she supposed to stop a torture session, anyway? What *was* a torture session? Like going for a massage? Was it a sexual thing that would get out of hand?

Even at this late hour, the streets of Vegas were still quite busy. She jostled past more people on the way back to her bike.

She saw the man with the facial scar again, a block from her bike.

She stopped. The doors to the Flamingo Casino were wide open, the sounds of the slot machines resonating onto the sidewalk. People cheered, and a bell sounded from somewhere inside.

The scarred man stood rock still, glaring at her. He appeared to be crying.

Standing the way he was in the middle of the casino floor, not moving, tears now running down his cheeks, really bothered her.

Was he upset that she had sent the text? What did she do that Vivian didn't have under control? And how did this guy know anything about it?

Vegas was all wrong. An eerie feeling crept up her back that she had set in motion events that would cost her. And the man with the scar not only knew what was going on but he was also troubled deeply by the weight of that knowledge.

Someone bumped into her, knocking her off balance.

"I'm so sorry," a man said. His wife smiled and reached out to Sarah.

"Excuse us," the woman said.

The couple kept walking along the sidewalk, the alcohol they had consumed working on them with each step they took.

Sarah looked back into the casino.

The man with the scar was gone.

Chapter 6

JAKE COLLINS STOOD IN front of the New York, New York Casino, and Hotel, staring up at the roller coaster as it raced by overhead, riders screaming. After it passed, he entered through the double set of doors and took in the casino floor as he patted the inside breast pocket that held his wallet. He panicked for a second, then patted the other breast pocket and felt the thick envelope with ten-thousand dollars in hundreds.

He felt safe in the casino with that much money. Security was everywhere, and there were gamblers with more on them than that sitting at the tables with their currency piled in chips for the world to see. No one would take a second look at him.

Just meet the girl, give her the cash, and get the hell out.

He'd have a lot to explain if he accidentally bumped into his brother while sitting with a twenty-something blonde.

Correction, a pregnant twenty-something blonde. Yeah, too much explaining.

He meandered through the slot machines, passed the bar

on his right, and headed for the escalators that would take him up to the bar where they were to meet.

His phone dinged. He pulled it out and saw he had a text from a number he didn't recognize. He opened the text.

Don't do it—keep the money.

He glanced up to see if anyone was watching him. Then he rechecked the number on his phone to see if it matched any of his contacts.

It didn't.

He had kept it a secret, even from Lana, which twisted his insides. He had never cheated on his wife except for one time, and yet he can't remember a single moment of it. He remembered being at that party, drinking too much, and shooting his mouth off. But waking up in bed with the woman, partially dressed, had scared the shit out of him.

He spent the first month back in Phoenix feeling like a lump of shit. If it had happened, he felt better knowing he had no intent. He could live with that. It wasn't an excuse, just reality. He never once intended to sleep with other women. If propositioned when sober, no matter who it was, what she looked like, or what state of undress the woman was in, he would always turn her down.

He had a lovely wife and child. No amount of fooling around was ever worth losing that.

But here he was, in Vegas, about to meet the girl that he not only cheated on his wife with but impregnated.

So who was the text from, and why send it?

He decided to reply. He sent a text asking the person to identify themselves.

After hitting send, he realized that it might be the girl he was about to meet. Maybe she had a change of heart and didn't want the abortion after all. It had to be her because the two of them were the only ones who knew about their little meeting tonight. They wouldn't send this text if she told someone close to her. They would want her to snatch the ten grand from the unsuspecting idiot from Phoenix.

"Shit," he mumbled under his breath. "What now?"

He moved off the aisle between card tables and sat on a chair at a closed roulette table.

Then he typed in another text.

Why don't you want the money? It could really help your situation. It's yours—no strings attached. Make the payment and save your life. You don't want the alternative.

He hit send.

It was time to meet with the girl, provided she showed up. After the text that she probably sent him, she might not.

He walked briskly to the escalators. Unless he took the stairs on the left, he would have to stand and wait until he got to the top. He decided on the escalator anyway.

Halfway up, his cell phone chirped again. Then it vibrated.

He yanked it out and checked call display. It was his brother, Bruce. Why would he call him? Jake had just arrived in Vegas. Could he have talked to Lana back in Phoenix?

There was no way he could take the call. Not this close to the meeting with the girl, whose name he had forgotten. He put his phone away and decided to call Bruce back after he got upstairs and was relaxing in his hotel room. It would be easier to talk to him when all this shit was done. He would have to call Lana back, too, as she had tried to reach him several times.

At the top of the escalator, he turned right. His phone

rang again as he passed the Houdini store, but he didn't pull it out or look at it. Probably his persistent brother. He knew he'd get lectured for not letting him know sooner that he was coming to Vegas, but he would deal with that when the time came. Right now, he needed to pay off the girl and get her out of his life. This needed to end. Tonight.

The door to the bar, Cowboy Ugly, was just ahead. A small line of people waited to get in. For a brief moment, he wondered if he was doing the right thing. He rationalized that even if she wasn't pregnant, she could call back and tell his wife all sorts of stories, and his marriage would fall apart anyway. Or they'd stay together, and he would spend the next dozen years repairing the damage caused. And forget about ever coming to Vegas for conventions again. That would be the end.

The girl had had the conference dates right, even the mole on his stomach that he had meant to get removed. He remembered her from that night, so if Lana were ever to ask about the pregnant girl in Vegas, there would be no way he could lie to her face without her seeing through it.

He hoped the girl would just go away after this and leave him and his family alone.

He got in line behind five women. They were giggling while discussing a guy named Steve, who was less than ample in size.

It didn't take long to get inside. His wait was less than five minutes. Once inside, he headed for the bar where women in cowboy boots danced on the countertop. The music was so loud, he couldn't imagine for a second how the two of them, once they met up, would be able to talk. He certainly wouldn't be able to hear his phone ring if his brother or Lana called him again. The excuse he had prepared was the three-card poker table—his favorite game. While sitting at the table, playing poker, he couldn't be on a cell phone. Since he was on a winning streak, he had to wait to call them back. They'd buy the excuse. It had happened before.

He ordered a double Southern Comfort and shot it back to help calm his nerves. He ordered another one to sip slowly while looking for the girl.

The dancer on the bar was finishing, the song coming to an end. People cheered, clapped, and went crazy as she finished with an exaggerated shake of her ass. His high school testosterone kicked in but warred with his committed adult married man side, which won out. He turned away, unable to visually take in the pleasure of a youthful leer.

Someone grabbed his arm. He almost jumped a foot and spilled his beverage over the top of his glass.

The girl. The pregnant girl. She was dressed in black, with heels. Her hair looked great, and her makeup had been applied just right.

What is this? A date?

His stomach felt like a brick resided there.

She shouted something, but he couldn't hear it. Then she gestured with a nod of her head for him to follow her and started walking toward the door.

He set his glass down on the bar and followed her. For the first time since he got the call a few days ago, he started to feel this was a shakedown. She said she was five months pregnant, yet there was no baby bump. In that tight black dress, he should be able to see it.

She led him out of the bar and past the line of people

waiting to get in.

"We won't be able to hear ourselves think in there," she said, then snorted as she giggled.

Being this close to her bothered him. It was all wrong. He had to watch that he didn't view her through a filter—one that made him see everything she did as suspect and conniving. If he did, he might say or do the wrong thing. This meeting had to end with him walking away clean.

"Come on, we can talk outside the hotel," she said.

They walked through the double doors outside to the walkway leading to the Excalibur Hotel. Chain-link fences had been erected on each side of the railing to stop suicidal jumpers.

Outside, they could talk in private with the noise of the traffic below and have people around as dozens traversed the walkway going back and forth between the two casinos.

"Where do we begin?" Jake asked.

"One sec," she said as she fidgeted in her purse.

He stepped back and kept a safe distance. He didn't know if she was about to pull mace out of her purse and blind him. Or worse, acid.

A pack of cigarettes came out, her hand clutching them as if it were a gold bar.

"Should you be doing that?" Jake asked. "You know, considering …"

She stopped what she was doing, the cigarette already in her mouth, the lighter halfway to her lips.

"You serious?"

"Well, yeah."

"I'm aborting, aren't I?"

"Of course, I mean, that's the idea. I guess I just thought

…" He let the words die as she brought the lighter to a flame and puffed on her cancer stick.

He still couldn't remember her name, or maybe he refused to. Spending too much time on the walkway wasn't what he had in mind. The odds that his brother would walk by and see him were low, but there was still that chance.

She turned to the fence and stared down at the vehicles passing below while puffing on her cigarette.

"So, how do you want to do this?" he asked.

She looked at him, her eyes a slit through the smoke leaving her mouth.

"I never wanted this to happen," she said.

"Me either."

That was a relief. They were starting on the right foot. Maybe this would go smoothly and not be so bad after all. He could lose the ten grand if that meant closing this chapter of his life. In fact, he wouldn't even miss the money. He'd consider it well spent.

As she pulled on the cigarette, her hands shook. "When I found out," she said, "I didn't know what to do."

"I can understand that."

She dropped her half-smoked cigarette and stomped on it. Then she turned to face him.

"I'm serious. This could really fuck up my life right now. It's hard enough to get jobs in Vegas. Imagine a pregnant waitress. Doesn't happen. This is the city of sex. Walking around showing that I've had some doesn't allow the customers to have the fantasies employers want."

"Yeah, I understand."

He had no idea where she was going with her rant. If she was saying that a baby bump ruined male fantasies at the workplace, Jake wondered what had happened to society.

"Anyway," she continued. "I want this done. Over. After looking into what I had to do, I decided to call you because I didn't have that kind of money."

"Fair enough. That's why I'm here."

"Take this." She offered his business card to him. "I won't be needing your contact information anymore." Then she pulled it back out of reach. "Providing you're going ahead with our plan. You are, aren't you?"

Jake nodded. "Of course. I think what you're doing is right for all of us." When he took the card, his hand shook as badly as hers. He felt sorry for her, trying to make it in Vegas, then getting pregnant and having an abortion. All he did was remove ten thousand from an account with hundreds of thousands in it and fly to his favorite city. Although after this, he would be a lot more careful in Vegas.

He stashed his card beside his wallet, remembering which pocket it was in this time.

"So, we agree?" she asked. "I get," she stopped and looked around conspiratorially, "money and an abortion, and you walk away, out of my life forever?"

"That was the agreement. I just hope you'll be okay."

"I will. Don't worry about me."

She fished in her purse again, then pulled out a stick of gum. She tossed it in her mouth without offering him any and started chewing. Her nervousness was catching.

"Well, did you bring it?" she asked.

"Right here." He padded his jacket.

"Is there anything else to say?" she asked.

"No. Not that I'm aware of."

"Then why are you waiting?" She held out her hand.

No one paid them any attention. The public walked by, oblivious to their meeting. His moist fingers touched the envelope. He pulled it out and placed it gently in her hand. It wasn't the money itself that bothered him; it was what the money was for, what it represented.

She jammed it into the bottom of her purse, zipped the top shut, and secured the purse under her arm, the strap linked around her shoulder.

"This means it ends here," Jake said, more a statement than a question.

She smiled, a devilish smile, like she and Satan had a secret. The devious smile spoke volumes about what she was thinking. His stomach did flip-flops. He wanted to back away and run but was held by her gaze.

"If you touch me, I'll scream rape," she whispered.

He put his hands up in defense. "I'm not going to touch you."

"If you shout at me, I will scream rape. Anything you do that I don't like, I'll have you in a Las Vegas jail before you can say *whore*. I'm seconds away from calling the cops right now. Are we clear?"

He backed up two steps. "Absolutely." He wanted to run but was held by her gaze. "But why? You have your money." He feared if he didn't hear her out, he would get a call in Phoenix when he got home. Not only would he be out ten grand, but he would also lose his marriage, too.

"I need another forty thousand." She shrugged. "Consider it silence money."

He shook his head. "No way. Too much. I can't do that kind of money. It'll get noticed."

She stepped toward him to close the distance he had

created.

"You can and you will, or your pretty little wife will hear all the sordid details. I will tell her about how you slipped inside me and fucked me all night. You fucked me so hard I couldn't walk right for a few days. It even hurt to pee. Now I'm pregnant and wanted her to know that your son will have a little brother soon. How about that?"

Fear turned to rage. His sweaty hands clenched uncontrollably. Suddenly he wanted to break her face. That would solve the problem. Put her in the hospital and threaten to do it again if she ever mentioned his name. Maybe that was what this little puke needed.

Somebody yelled behind him. Revelers walked by, greeting everyone they passed. It broke Jake's moment of focused rage. He returned to the here and now and started rationalizing forty more thousand.

"I will leave you alone after that. One-hundred percent. You have my guarantee once I have the whole fifty. Anything less, your life becomes hell. These aren't empty threats. This is just the way it is." She spat on the ground. He realized that she had just spit her gum out. "You fucked me and got me pregnant. Now you pay for that. Too bad. That's life."

"Okay, okay, keep your voice down."

"Meet me back here tomorrow, same time. Bring the money. Do we have a deal?"

He nodded. There was no time to think, there was nothing else he could do. He had to agree, or this woman could walk away and use a cell phone to call his wife, virtually ending his life as he knew it. Sure, she handed his business card back, but she would've recorded the information on it somewhere. Stunned and shocked, he stood speechless with a dry bitterness in his mouth.

"Good," she said. "Now, hug me."

"What?"

"Hug me. My boyfriend is watching. When you hug me, it signals to him that we have a deal. If you walk away, he calls your wife. So I advise you to hug me and make it look real. Make it look like we are fuck buddies. I want a close, intimate hug."

He stepped in, wondering what he had gotten himself into. She moved into him and wrapped her arms inside his jacket, resting her head on his chest. For all intents and purposes, they looked like a couple who had just resolved a conflict and were ready to head back up to their room.

He felt the warmth of her body against his and instantly thought of Lana. It saddened him to think she was home with Michael, and he was in Vegas hugging a pretty blonde that he'd had sex with. He felt three inches tall and wanted to crawl into a two-inch hole.

He made to pull away. She threw her arms out and then wrapped them tighter around his waist.

"No. Longer. We have to make sure he doesn't call your wife. If he does, we both lose. Just another few seconds."

He hugged her and waited.

Then she pulled away fast like he'd bitten her. She swung around quickly, her purse arcing on its strap, and walked away.

"Same time, same place," she said over her shoulder. "Tomorrow night. Be there or lose your life."

He stood in her wake, dumbfounded. The seriousness of the situation spilled over him, and he almost crumbled to the ground. He turned around in a daze, entered the New York,

New York Casino doors, and returned to the escalators.

He could talk to Lana, save them forty grand. What would she say? What would she do? Maybe he could convince her that he was being scammed? Although, if she believed that, she would recommend they bring Bruce in on it and have the girl arrested. No, that wouldn't work.

He ruffled his hair and loosened his shirt a button. It had gotten very hot in the casino. At the bottom of the escalator, he wended his way toward the elevators by Gallagher's Steakhouse that would take him up to his room.

He would take the night to think about it. Sleep on it. Maybe he'd have whiskey brought up to the room.

At the casino's cashier, he could make a debit withdrawal for the amount of money the girl was looking for. They did it all the time for high rollers. He just needed to think about it.

Near the elevators, he removed his jacket. Sweat had marked his white shirt under his arms, but he didn't care who saw it. It was just too damn hot.

Something was wrong with his jacket. It felt lighter. He pushed the button for the elevator to come down and patted his jacket. It was lighter because the money was gone. Then he realized what the problem was.

His wallet was gone, too.

Frantically, he reached inside his breast pocket. The wallet was gone, as was the business card she had given him back that he had placed beside the wallet. Only his cell phone remained in his smaller cell phone pocket.

"For fuck's sake." He slammed a foot on the floor.

There was no way he could run after her. She was long gone. The only way to solve this was to meet her at the same time tomorrow night and get his wallet back.

She'll be surprised when I don't have the money because the card to access the money is inside my fucking wallet.

He wondered why he forgot to ask her if she was the one who had sent him the text. If it wasn't her, then who did?

His phone rang. He pulled it out as the elevator door opened.

It was his brother calling again. He was in no mood to talk to anybody, let alone his brother. He jammed the phone away and stepped toward the elevator.

"Jake!" someone called.

Just as he was about to enter the elevator, he saw his brother running toward him, cell phone in hand.

Jake jumped on the elevator and hit the close-door button, praying it closed before Bruce got there.

It did and instantly began rising.

The elevator was empty. To avoid Bruce finding out what floor he was staying on, he hit two other numbers. On his floor, he got off and ran to his room.

Inside the room, he hung the DO NOT DISTURB sign on the door, closed it, and leaned his back against it.

Then he slipped to the floor, wondering what he was going to do.

He lifted his jacket to his face and cried into it.

Chapter 7

MARK STEAD SAT IN the back of the cab, shaking so much he wondered if he could hold his piss. He had no idea who the crazy girl with the gun was. Or why she made him send a text about keeping the money.

His phone had announced an incoming text a few moments ago. Of course, it was the person he'd texted asking who he was and something about the money saving his life.

At the airport, he would reread it and decide what to say or even if he was going to respond.

The cab turned off the Vegas strip, drove behind the Bally's and Paris Hotels, and turned right, headed back toward McCarren International Airport.

Mark needed to leave Las Vegas or face Maxwell. Him and his buddy, Tyrone, had gambled too much, drank too much, and snorted the rest up their noses. He didn't care what Tyrone would do, but Mark was getting the fuck out.

He had enough money stashed away for a plane ticket to Mexico. He could live a few months down there without working. After that, he would figure out what to do next. Getting as far away as possible from Maxwell Ramsey was all he could think about for now.

There was no way they could pay the money back. When Tyrone was running for Big John, they were *rolling in the deep*, as they liked to call the wads of cash. But now they were all out of deep and only in deep shit.

The cab banked hard to the left through a yellow light. Mark could already see the lights of airplanes lining up to land. To his right, a plane ascended overhead, leaving Las Vegas.

He smiled. Leaving Las Vegas. Who would've thought he would leave the hustling, bustling city of sin?

He was either leaving it in a plane or a casket.

He leaned back in the seat and closed his eyes to rest. It took another five minutes until the cab pulled up in front of the terminal. Mark paid, gave the driver a generous tip, and closed the door behind him.

He took a deep breath, inhaling the damp heat after the rain. It might be the last time he stood on Vegas soil.

The automatic doors opened, and four large men stepped out of the terminal, heading his way.

He frowned. Maxwell's men? No way. They couldn't know where he was. Two hours ago, he called Maxwell and told him he was on his way to make a payment. No one would be looking for him for another forty-five minutes yet. By then, he would be through security and waiting to board his plane to Mexico.

The men got closer. He recognized one of them. They *were* coming for him. He turned to run and alert airport security, but three men stepped up behind him.

"Going somewhere, Mark?" the biggest one said.

"Picking up a friend," tumbled out of his mouth.

"Ahh, how nice. You're going to miss your friend, though. Maybe he can catch a cab into the city. Maxwell wants to see you. Apparently," he made an exaggerated attempt to look at his watch, "you've got an appointment with him in just over a half hour. Perfect timing. You won't be late now. We all know how Ramsey hates it when folks are late."

The four men who had emerged from the terminal had stopped behind him now. All seven men surrounded him in a circle. There was no way out. No excuses. There was just too much muscle. He would have to go with them. Probably never see Mexican soil now, or any other country's, except for the dark hard-packed soil found six feet under the Vegas lights.

The big man who spoke to him pointed at a waiting stretch limo.

"Do I have to ask twice?" His voice had developed a hard edge.

Mark put one foot in front of the other, walked over, and entered the open door of the limo. Two men entered with him, and the car started moving. The rest of the men stayed behind, probably to monitor other debtors making mad dashes for the airport.

How many fucking people does Maxwell employ?

Then it occurred to him that he could work his debt off. Maybe Maxwell could give him menial jobs as payback for his debt. He'd do whatever Maxwell wanted to get this behind them. Torturing him, or worse, killing him, wouldn't pay the debt.

Then he thought about hope and how finicky a friend it was. As finicky as Lady Luck. He sat in Maxwell's limo on his way to a heavy beating or death and entertained the idea that he would be rewarded with a job.

Hilarious.

The drugs, the gambling, and the bimbos were over for him. You could do that on your own dime, but when you were addicted to pussy and the cash that attracts it—once you run out of cash, you have to borrow it, and Maxwell loves to hand out money. Maybe because he loves collecting it a little too much.

"Where are we going?" Mark asked.

"Your funeral."

The two thugs laughed.

"Classy."

"Whatchoo say, mutherfucker?" the bigger one snapped. "Say it again, say it again."

"I just want you to take me to Maxwell since we have a meeting. Maxwell and I need to talk."

"Oh, don't worry, you fucking pig. You gonna talk all right. You gonna talk real good. You might even sing."

He sat back and waited out the ride. There was no use discussing business with hired thugs with egos bigger than their biceps. He was already intimidated. The funny thing was, the two idiots across from him didn't know it. They felt they had to keep trying to scare him.

The limo drove away from the strip and into the city. Finally, on the west side of the city limits, the limo stopped in front of a linen warehouse of some kind.

"Out," the bigger one commanded.

Maxwell had always met with him in hotel rooms at

various casinos. Once, it was the Mirage, and another time, Mandalay Bay. Mark had always assumed that was because Ramsey needed to be near casinos that had cashiers to get the money he needed to hand over.

Meeting Maxwell Ramsey at a warehouse on the west side of Vegas at this late hour only meant one thing.

Mark was in trouble.

He hadn't heard of Maxwell having anyone killed before, but he wouldn't put it past the man. At least he looked the part with the dreadlocks and the tats. He even had a tattoo on his face. Some Italian symbols. He always wondered who would put a tattoo on their face unless they'd been to prison —or a mental hospital.

The men led him to the side door of the warehouse. The big man opened the door and stood to the side.

"Can't we talk out here?" Mark asked.

The man holding the door stared at him and waited. The other guy stood rock-still behind him, his arm buried in his jacket, no doubt holding a gun. He didn't want another gun in his face on the same day, so he stepped inside.

The linen factory had row after row of large bales of fabric. Huge machines lined the back wall with what looked like strings attached every which way, resembling colorful spider webs.

The men led him to an open area by a lunchroom door at the back. Security night lights were on with one large dome light directly above them.

A movement to the left caught his eye as more men joined them. Maxwell wasn't among them.

"Where's Maxwell?" Mark asked. "We're supposed to meet at ten."

Something hit him from behind, which knocked him flat onto the cold metal floor. Pain shot up from his leg in a rush. He screamed and grabbed for his leg.

Two men jumped on him and attached something to his ankles. Within seconds his ankles were secured to some kind of wooden trap that was connected to ropes.

The big man from the limo held a baseball bat.

The back of his left knee felt two sizes too big. He prayed nothing was broken.

"Come on, guys," Mark pleaded.

"Fuck you. Shut up."

One of the men moved off to the side and spun a large wheel connected to the wall. The contraption on his ankles was pulled up into the air by the ropes.

"Hey, guys, come on."

His feet rose until only his shoulders remained on the metal floor.

"Guys, is this really necessary? Maxwell and I go back. We did a lot of business together. When he finds out you did this, he's gonna be pissed."

The big one stepped into view.

"Somehow, I don't think so. He's the one who ordered this."

"What?"

Mark was in serious trouble. If Maxwell knew he was trying to run and had these guys pick him up, he didn't know if he would last the night. They may not kill him, but Mark couldn't handle a beating. Pain was his enemy, and it always won.

Sweat beaded on his forehead. "Look, tell Maxwell that I'll get the money. Please, you don't have to do this."

He still hadn't used the bathroom, and now the piss he had trouble holding in the cab on the way to the airport spilled out and down his stomach, trickling to the floor by his chest.

A man stepped close to his feet and yanked on his running shoes, pulling them off. Then he ripped off Mark's socks.

"Sensitive feet?" the guy asked.

Mark nodded fast and hard. "Yeah, yeah. Listen, please …"

Out of nowhere, the man produced a whip with something shiny on the tails. He swung the whip, snapped it twice in the air, then whipped it across the soles of Mark's feet. Mark gasped, his body went rigid, his eyes wide at the instant shock of pain that coursed through him. Then he shouted and writhed under the restraints, trying his best to wiggle free and getting nowhere.

He screamed again and again and tried to perform a sit-up to reach his ankles and unlock them, but he couldn't quite make it that high.

Blood trickled over the edge of his heel and dripped down to the floor below. He cried so hard he needed to wipe his face.

"Dude, you better get your breathing under control before you hyperventilate," the big one holding the bat said.

The pain was absolutely unbearable. Like nothing he'd ever felt.

"I can stop this," the man said. "But you gotta help me first."

"Okay, okay, whatever you want," Mark shouted. "Just please, no more feet. No more feet. I'll do whatever you ask."

"Where were you going tonight?" He held up a finger. "And no lies."

"Um, I … ahh." There was no way he could tell them the truth. No way. "I was picking up a friend at the airport—"

The whip cut him off. It slashed across the arch of his feet. It hit so hard that he wondered briefly if his feet were torn in half. Blood didn't just trickle down this time. It shot in the air, following the whip's arc.

Mark screamed until his voice was hoarse. Stars rolled throughout his vision. The room grew dark. He was sure he was about to pass out.

Suddenly a bucket of water was dumped on his head, and he was wide awake again, gasping for breath, swallowing the excess liquid. It tasted of metal.

"Good, you're back with us."

Mark clenched his teeth against the pain and looked at each man in turn. He wanted their faces forever in his memory. If he got out of this alive, each man would die in his sleep when he healed. Pliers to their dicks would be the easy way out for these scum.

"Are you ready to stop lying, or would you rather we just amputate your feet?"

Words he never thought he would hear. They sounded so horrible, his stomach clenched, and he vomited, angling his head to the side, so he didn't choke on it.

The big man stepped away. He ordered more water and one of the other men to clean up the mess.

"There's no fucking way I'm talking to this piece of shit with the smell of bile in my nose," the big man shouted.

His feet grew numb as they cleaned the puke up. If only

it was over and they didn't touch his feet again, then maybe he could make it out of this.

Once they finished the cleanup, the big man pulled a chair over and sat down close to Mark's head, the baseball bat across his thighs.

"Deal time. I ask the questions, and you give honest answers. For each lie, you get three whacks from the whip. Count 'em, three whacks. If you keep lying, I increase the whacks to five. Eventually, I'll pull your pants off, and we will hit you fifty times in the balls until you have none left. Then we'll see who wants to lie to me."

Mark couldn't find his voice. He nodded so hard that his head banged against the floor.

"Good. Now, put your hands under your ass."

"Why?" Mark asked, his voice restored to a squeak.

"Do it or be whipped."

Mark did as he was told. The big man leaned in close and rifled through Mark's pockets, pulling out the printed itinerary for Mexico and his cell phone and wallet. After pulling the five thousand out of Mark's wallet, he smiled down at him.

"Maxwell is going to be pissed," the big man said.

"That's my payment to him," Mark spit out. "We had a deal."

"The deal was for ten grand."

"Tyrone has the other half."

The big man was shaking his head. "No, he doesn't. Tyrone's dead."

"What?" Mark couldn't believe it. "How? Why?"

The man scrunched his eyebrows at Mark. "You really are a stupid motherfucker."

"It was only fifty thousand." Mark felt shock settling in over his system. "Maxwell kills people for unpaid debts?" he asked out loud, more to himself.

"Number one, it's more than fifty grand. Number two, Maxwell won't tolerate disrespect. Tyrone was a message. When news hits the street, debts will be easier to collect. And three, you're the second part of the message."

"What?" he asked. Then louder, "What!" He yanked on his feet and only succeeded in adding to the pain.

"We left him in that trailer we found him in." The big man leaned in close. "First, we cut his tongue out and then his eyes. Can't speak, can't see. Then we did things to him while he was still alive that you wouldn't wish on the man who raped your wife."

Shock set in. Mark would never have borrowed the money if he had known this was coming. He couldn't believe Tyrone was dead. They'd known each other since they lived on the same street when they were eight years old. Regrets were horrible at a time like this.

"Aha, a plane ticket to Cancun for tonight, and it's in your name." He looked down and met Mark's eyes. "Picking up a friend, eh? Who do you think Maxwell Ramsey is? You think you could take his money, have fun with it and then just fly off to Mexico? You are so small time it makes my head hurt." The man looked around at his comrades. "Can you guys believe this punk was going to run away?" He looked back down at Mark. "You are so dumb, but we're here to smarten you up. Fucking idiot."

He clicked Mark's cell phone buttons, scrolling through it while Mark tried to keep his breathing under control. He snuck a peek at his feet. The blood had slowed, but it still dripped off the edges of both heels. The man with the whip stood passively off to the side, waiting for his chance to go another round.

"Whoa, wait a minute. What's this?" The big man set the bat down and got to his feet. "A text from someone. Listen, it says, *Why don't you want the money? It could really help your situation. It's yours—no strings attached. Make the payment and save your life. You don't want the alternative.* And it's a reply from a text sent from this phone that says, *don't do it—keep the money.*" He stood over Mark's head, looking down at him. "Who you be telling to keep the money? It sure looks like from their reply that they be willing to give it to you. Are you a stupid motherfucker? I mean, seriously?"

"I can explain that."

"Oh yeah, sure you can. Go ahead." He waved at the rest of the men. "I'm sure we all want to hear this one."

"Some chick walked up off the street and ordered me to send that first text. After I left her and jumped in the cab to go to the airport, I received the other text. The one you just read."

"Some chick, huh? Just made you send a text?"

"I swear. She had long brown hair and a biker jacket of some kind. She was quite the looker. When I refused, she pulled a gun and made me send that text."

"Do you know how crazy you sound?"

"I swear on my life, man. That is exactly what happened."

"You're saying a random chick walked up to you on the street, pulled a gun, and made you text someone?"

"Exactly."

The men assembled around laughed.

"And you don't know who you texted?"

"No. I have no idea who that is."

"Wow, I've heard some crazy shit before, but that takes the cake."

"It's true," Mark pleaded.

"Yeah, of course, it's true. I have girls walk up to me, pull guns and make me text things all the time."

The big guy stepped away from Mark's head and handed the phone off to another man. "Find out who owns that phone number. Triangulate it. Call your buddy at the phone company. I want a name and location within the hour. If this guy has Maxwell's money and Mark is too stupid to accept it, I want the fucking money. Now go."

The big man turned back to Mark as the other guy ran off with his cell phone.

"Now, what to do with you." He rubbed his chin in an exaggerated expression of thought. "Guys, take off his clothes. Do it now."

Mark writhed under their hands as his shirt was torn from him. His jeans wouldn't rip as easily, so one of the men used a knife to slice them off. Then they tore his underwear from him. Mark cried and pleaded. He begged for mercy. He swore he could get the money. They just had to give him a chance.

"I'm not a money manager," the big guy said. "Look at me. Do you think I manage money for other people?"

Mark shook his head frantically.

"Right. I was hired to do a job, and that job was to collect a debt from Tyrone Percy and Mark Stead. Tyrone didn't have it in cash, so he paid a heavier price. You have some cash, so you won't lose your eyes or tongue, but I can tell you this, your payment involves a broom handle and a lot of problems with shitting for the next month. And I'm not just talking about the tip of the handle." He looked around at the men. "Hey guys, you think he can manage the whole thing?" The men all agreed Mark could handle it all.

"Great. Get me the broom."

Mark wished he was dead. He mentally called out to God and asked for mercy.

"While we wait, whip him again. But not just the feet. Whip his legs, chest, and face. When I go to the movies, I want to see blood. Tonight is a special presentation of gore and violation." He clapped his hands together, madness behind his eyes. "Ohhh, I'm going to enjoy this."

The whip came down across his thighs and then stomach before he even got the first long scream out.

Chapter 8

Kristi Raine paid the cab driver and started the long walk into the trailer park. She was so happy with herself, so happy that she had managed to make a deal that would get her and Tyrone out from under Maxwell's world, that she gave the cab driver a hundred-dollar tip.

She giggled because he probably thought she was a dancer or a street walker the way she was dressed. The cash she pulled out of the envelope while in the back seat had to be the most she had ever seen in her entire life. She hadn't opened Jake Collins's wallet yet. That was for later when they were together. That way, Tyrone could tell her what credit cards he would use and which ones to throw away.

After pulling out all that cash in the taxi, in case the driver had seen it, she had asked him to drop her off at the road. That way, he would never know which trailer she lived in. They'd be out by tomorrow and long gone, but she still wanted to be cautious and not take any chances. Vegas was a tough town. In the restaurant where she worked, she learned of a taxi-cab scam that once played out. Dozens of drivers were arrested. At least, that's what she remembered.

You can't trust no one.

She picked up her step and skipped past darkened trailers, turned a corner, and started down the row that led to hers. That night's score would probably top most of what Tyrone had done in the past year.

He'd better be happy about this.

She only hoped he wasn't passed out or drunk. He should be awake and waiting for her so he could share in the good news.

Tomorrow night they would get the rest of the money from Jake, and they could leave Las Vegas. Just like Tyrone had promised.

A dog barked somewhere in the trailer park. Someone's TV blared out an open window. The air was still, already warmer than earlier when it rained. Small puddles were all that remained of the rain.

A light was on in their living room.

Good, he's still up.

This was one of the few times she had done something for him. Since they had been together, Tyrone had been running for Big John and then borrowing from Maxwell so he could gamble. In the past few weeks, everything had crashed down around them. The threat of violence became a reality. Tyrone received his last warning. He had set a meet-up to pay Maxwell an installment, but Tyrone didn't have it.

Mark Stead was supposed to come up with enough to cover the two of them. They had worked together in the past. She knew they were connected as far back as high school or something, but now none of that mattered. Not with the money she had on her. They could pay Maxwell if Tyrone wanted, or they could leave Vegas behind and forget about Maxwell Ramsey forever.

Whatever Ty decided to do, she was game. They would have to wait until tomorrow night to do it, though. Jake was bringing them a lot more money—get-set-up-in-a-new-town money.

She hopped up the steps and pulled out her key, then stopped. The door to the trailer sat ajar. Light seeped through the small opening.

"Ty?" she called as she pushed open the door. "Ty, you here?"

Nothing looked amiss except, of course, the garbage all over the place. The pizza boxes and empty beer cans were still scattered everywhere. The TV was on mute, a car chase on the screen.

She stepped all the way in and shut the door behind her.

"Tyrone, you here?"

It would really piss her off if he had gone somewhere. After all she went through, he had better be home and waiting for the good news.

She looked down the hall and saw from under the door that the bathroom light was on. Ty hated to talk when he was in there.

"Sorry, baby. I didn't know."

She pulled out all the cash and walked over to the coffee table. She brushed the contents off the table to the floor and then fanned out all the hundreds, making a pretty picture for Ty when he came out of the bathroom.

Then she set Jake's wallet on the kitchen counter. Once Tyrone counted the cash, she would show him the wallet.

She walked past the bathroom door and into the small bedroom. It was time to get ready for a night of hard, rough sex. That much money would make Ty horny, for sure.

She slipped off her shoes and tossed them in the corner. Her arm still hurt too much to get to the zipper on her dress, so she pulled it over her head. Halfway up, it got stuck. She wrenched on it and heard it rip somewhere.

"Fuck."

She grabbed the hem, gripped it tightly, and yanked hard. It flipped off her head, pulling her hair slightly, but it was off.

With a quick flick of the wrist, she tossed it in the far corner of the messy bedroom. She could get another favorite dress now. They were no longer broke.

"Hey, Ty, how long you gonna be? I gotta nice surprise for you."

Her figure in the dresser's mirror still looked good. Standing in her small lace panties, she moved her hips back and forth.

Baby-making hips, she thought. *Maybe Tyrone will want to settle down now—start a family.*

It occurred to her that she hadn't heard a single noise from the bathroom. No shower or flush of the toilet. And why had the front door been open? She understood if he were going to be in there a long time, he wouldn't want her to have to use her key, but now she was getting worried.

She moved to the bathroom door quietly and placed an ear against it. The sound of running water was loud and clear.

She ran her hands down her near-naked body and swayed her hips again.

"Hey, Ty, come on out. I've got money and some pussy for you."

After a moment and no response, she knocked on the door.

"Ty, at least say something. You okay in there?"

Nothing.

"Ty?"

She tried the door. It opened. Cautiously, so that she didn't see anything that would embarrass him, she eased the door open and peeked inside. Her foot stepped in thick red liquid on the tile floor. Before she could stop, she slipped and fell, banging her knee on the porcelain toilet bowl.

"Ah, fuck, that hurts." She breathed in and gagged. "What the hell's that smell?"

The floor was covered, and the red liquid was coming from the shower stall. The curtain was closed, but the water still ran slowly.

"Ty, you're scaring me. Is this blood?"

She brought her hands to her nose and gagged again; the slickness smeared over her skin where she had fallen and rolled in it, wearing only her panties.

Carefully, she got to her feet and stepped closer to the shower stall, holding her breath.

"Ty?" she asked loud enough to be heard.

She pulled the shower curtain back and screamed.

Tyrone wasn't in the form of a human body anymore. He was chunked up in pieces, his head sitting atop the mutilated body. In the second that image entered her consciousness, she knew it would never leave. Whoever had done this had left the water running to help move the body's liquids down the drain, but part of his abdomen plugged the drainage hole, and blood had seeped over the stall's small lip.

She covered her mouth, cutting off a scream as she

backed away. Her shoulder blades bumped the wall, and she jumped as if someone was behind her. She spun and tried to run out the door but lost her balance on the slick floor and landed on her side hard, rolling in Tyrone's blood. She screamed as loud as she could, trying to keep her sanity contained but failing.

She crawled from the bathroom, entered the living room, and pulled herself up with the side of the kitchen counter. A couple of steps, and she was at the door.

It never occurred to her to use the phone to call for help. Instead, she ran outside in her panties, covered in Tyrone's blood, to get as far away from the trailer as possible.

As she ran through the trailer park, she screamed hysterically until she collapsed near the road.

Chapter 9

"WHY WOULD YOUR BROTHER run like that?" Mara asked.

Bruce moved away from the elevator and watched the lights. The lift stopped on three different floors. Now he didn't know what floor his brother was staying on, and it was clear his brother didn't want him to know.

What the fuck is Jake up to?

Russell's warning came back to him. If he didn't do what Sarah Roberts asked, his brother would be in trouble. At least, that was how he remembered it. He hadn't written it down or memorized it, but message or no message, however he looked at it, Jake Collins was in some kind of trouble. This wasn't normal behavior for his brother.

"Follow me," Bruce said.

"Where to?" Mara asked.

"Just come on."

Bruce moved out into the casino area and headed to the main desk. People converged in a row at the counter, waiting to check in, luggage behind them.

Bruce flashed his badge at the side of the counter and then moved to an empty wicket. The attendants were always well-dressed at Vegas hotels. A young woman with a ponytail nodded at them and stepped up to greet them.

"I'm Detective Bruce Collins, and this is Detective Mara Munro. We're looking for one of your guests. A man named Jake Collins."

"And you know he's staying with us?" she asked as she turned and typed on a keyboard in front of a computer.

"Yes." A short, clipped answer.

She stopped typing, rested a hand on her hip, and faced Bruce. "We have a strict policy of privacy here. I would love to help out the police, but I would need paperwork of some kind to release any information about our guests."

Bruce saw through her stance and recognized how nervous she was. It might be in the company manual to be discreet about the guests, but the company manual wouldn't help when faced with the police and having to deny them.

"I understand. All I'm looking for is what room my brother is staying in. You saw my ID. Jake is my brother. I want to surprise him—"

"Susan, everything okay here?"

A tall woman with hair forced back into a bun so tight the skin on her face was taut, stepped up behind the clerk.

"Everything's fine, Rose. They were just asking—"

"I got this," Rose said and edged her way in front of Susan, who moved away and slipped through a door, disappearing into the back.

"Now, how can I help you?" Rose asked.

"I just saw my brother in the casino. He used the elevators by Gallagher's and went up to his room. I just want his room number so I can surprise him."

"And your name is?"

"Detective Bruce Collins. This is Detective Mara Munro."

"Can I see some ID, please?"

Bruce tried not to show impatience when he pulled out his ID. Rose examined them as if she was looking for a typo in the text.

"I'm sorry," she said. "We can't help you."

"Excuse me?" Bruce asked.

"Is this official police business?"

Bruce snuck a glance at Mara and then back at Rose. "No, it isn't."

"Then I can't help you. Was there anything else?"

"All we want is his room number," Bruce said.

"Let me record your badge numbers. Isn't it the law I can ask for them, and you have to give them to me?"

"Why the cold shoulder?" Bruce asked.

"You come in here and announce that you're a detective. When I asked if this was official police business, you said no. Since this is *un*official, why say you're a detective? Are you trying to use, or should I say, misuse your title of detective to get what you want?"

"Holy shit, woman. Overreact much?"

She leaned in close. "My ex-husband was a cop. He did it all the time. I know the laws and will not bend over because you say you're a cop." She pulled back. "Now, if you don't want me to file an *official* complaint with your department, move along. Our privacy standards protect our guests. You will have to call your *family* member and locate him through other channels. Private channels. You're a detective, right?"

Rose looked away and started typing on a computer.

Bruce grabbed Munro's arm and walked her out of earshot.

"What the fuck was that?" he asked.

"I'm just happy you didn't smack her. Just our luck to get Medusa after her marriage broke down to Satan's brother." She shrugged. "What're we going to do now?"

"I'll call Jake, text him, and then call him again. He'll answer. If not, I'll call Lana back in Phoenix and see if she knows what his room number is."

He retrieved his phone, then stopped. The snarky woman behind the counter, Rose, still watched him.

"I'm calling in for the search warrant," he said, then offered her his best fuck-you smile.

Rose shrugged and glanced away.

"Bruce, don't be so juvenile," Munro said with a smirk.

His phone rang in his hand.

"Hello."

"Detective Bruce Collins?"

"Yeah, you got him."

"This is Detective Mackey, homicide. I have a crime scene you might want to come see."

He looked at Munro, who scowled.

"Why would I want to see it?"

"Do you know a man named Tyrone Percy?"

"Name rings a bell. If it's the same guy I'm thinking about, he does small jobs for Big John. Tied in with Maxwell Ramsey, too."

"Not anymore."

"What do you mean?"

"Tyrone is deceased. He was found in the shower of his

trailer cut up in four pieces. According to witnesses, his girlfriend found him and ran out of the trailer screaming her head off."

"Okay, why tell me? Who has the lead on this one?"

"We found something you might be interested in at the scene."

Bruce stared at Munro, covered the mouthpiece, and whispered, "One sec." Then he moved away from the gamblers and into an alcove by the escalator that led up to the second-floor games room.

"What did you find?" he asked.

"Ten thousand dollars in cash and a wallet with ID in it for a man named Jake Collins."

"What?" He couldn't believe what he was hearing.

"Kristi Rain, the girlfriend, claims she scammed a man named Jake Collins into giving it to her. His whole wallet is here, ID and everything. That's Jake Collins from Phoenix, Arizona. Got his address right here. Your card is in with his ID. Thought maybe you wanted in on this as it looks like he's family and all."

"Give me the address, and I'll be right over."

Bruce wrote it all down, then slapped his phone closed.

"Munro, I need your help."

She nodded. "Who was that? What'd they want?"

"Homicide. They got a body. Funny thing is, my brother's ID showed up at the murder scene."

"Oh. That can't be good."

"I know. We can't let Jake out of our sight. I need you to sit outside the elevator bank by Gallagher's and watch for him to come down. When he does, nab him and bring him to me. In the meantime, I'll grab a warrant to get Jake's room number. I have a reason now."

"You got it. Where you gonna be first?"

"At the scene of Tyrone Percy's murder."

They started walking.

"Tyrone Percy's dead?" Munro asked.

"Sounds like it. Brutal too. Dismembered."

"Oh shit, somebody was angry. Always a little more personal when it's like that."

"Yeah."

They got to the area where Munro could watch the elevators.

"Go in the bar over there. Sit in the corner. You'll be able to see if he comes out from there."

"Got it. Go."

Without another word, Bruce ran for his car.

Whatever game Russell Anderson was playing by coming into their station and saying that Jake was in Vegas and in trouble, Bruce was determined to play it out until the end.

Then he would arrest Russell and put him in jail right where he was supposed to be.

Nobody fucks with the Collins family.

Chapter 10

SARAH TURNED OFF HER bike and swung her leg in a wide arc to dismount. She eased off her helmet and swung her hair back.

Vivian had given her a message moments after she had gotten to her bike. The message had arrived in a new way Vivian had started using. Sarah wouldn't pass out completely as she had before. Now that she carried an iPhone, Vivian could take over Sarah's arm long enough to type the message into her phone. The few times Sarah had done this, it simply looked like she was very focused on texting. Mentally, she felt out of it for a moment, but then came to seconds later, and her phone's screen had the message.

An address for a warehouse in the west end lit up on her screen. She had typed it into her map feature and was directed to the area. According to her phone, she was one block from the warehouse. The rest of the distance would be on foot as she didn't want her presence known too early.

She checked the time. She was supposed to have stopped

the torture session five minutes ago.

"Shit."

As she jogged down the side road, she wondered what state the tortured person would be in if she showed up too late.

At the corner, by the road, she dimmed the light on her phone and checked for directions.

The building she needed was a linen factory across the street. At this late hour, it was the only building with cars out front. Seven vehicles were parked on the side by an access door.

After a quick check of her gun, she stuck it in the back of her pants, flexed her fingers, looked both ways, and crossed the road. Now on the fabric factory's property, she bent low and ran for the shelter of the building. Once she reached the wall, she stopped, calmed her breathing, and listened.

Voices emanated from inside. Someone shouted something. A man laughed. Then she heard a smack of some kind, and another man screamed.

"Damn it."

The door was twenty feet away. If she walked in that one, they could all be right there. Vivian hadn't mentioned how many she would encounter.

Could have used more direction on this one, Sis.

She hated to go in blind, but the torture she was supposed to stop would continue if she wasted time looking for another way in. And what if she couldn't find another way in? Then she would have wasted valuable time.

"Fuck it," she whispered.

The gun came out of the back of her pants with ease. She flipped off the safety and moved to the door to try the handle.

It was unlocked. She put her ear to it and listened. The inside noises were a little distance away, but that didn't mean someone wasn't parked on the other side of the door.

With her fingers loosely wrapped on the door handle, she edged it open slowly, the tip of her weapon aimed chest high. Once the door was open a foot, she could see enough to know no one stood guard.

She slipped inside and closed the door behind her quietly. The building was laid out with rows and rows of fabric in large, thick rolls like oversized carpets. Along the nearest aisle, the factory opened up into an area with large machines.

Someone screamed from the corner on her right. Staying low, she ran across to the first aisle and pushed her back into a fabric roll, her gun aimed at the ceiling.

On the other side of the row, she guessed the building's occupants to be about three rows away. Men were discussing something about an address.

"I got it," one guy said.

"Where?" This voice was louder, deeper.

"The cell phone belongs to a guy named Jake Collins. He's staying at the New York Hotel tonight, booked in for one night, according to my guy."

"You got the room number?" Deep Voice asked.

"Yup."

"Good. Go. Get all the money he has. If it's more than the debt this fuck owes, take it all. Consider it interest. Then rough him up. If you don't hospitalize this Jake asshole, I hospitalize you. Got it."

"Yes, Boss."

"Get out of my sight and get the job done."

Sarah listened and debated if she should stop the men

from leaving the warehouse. But her instructions were to stop a torture at this location. With men leaving, it would prove easier to do that job. To stop the roughing up of someone at the New York Hotel wasn't what Vivian had asked of her.

Footsteps echoed closer. She got down on her knees and then her stomach. The bottom of the racks that held the fabric rolls was two feet off the ground. She slid under one like sliding under a car.

Four men ran by her aisle just as she hid. They hit the door and exited fast, slamming it behind them.

She only hoped the torture that was about to happen to this Jake guy at the New York Hotel had nothing to do with the torture she was supposed to stop here. Otherwise, she would fail Vivian, and the consequences of that were always bad.

She crawled out from her hiding spot and got to her feet.

Deep Voice shouted, "Where the fuck is my broom?"

She started along the aisle, working her way to the large machines at the heart of the building. Other voices echoed off the walls, but they were too low to discern what was being said. At the corner, she peeked around the edge. A man stood by the wall, his back to her, three aisles up. Something held his attention to his right.

She kissed the tip of her gun, said a quick word to Vivian, then stepped out into the open.

"I found a broom," someone yelled behind her.

She spun around. The man hadn't seen her yet. He had emerged from a row three aisles away. His head was down as he swiveled the brush end off the broom. She hopped back into the aisle she had just jumped out of. Catching her breath, she waited, her weapon ready.

He moved past her position, and she fell in step behind him. At the second he detected her, she brought the gun down, the handle whacking the back of his head. Knocking a man out cold took a lot, so she forced all her strength into the downswing. He crumpled to the floor at her feet.

Before the broom handle could clatter to the floor, she snatched it from his grip, catching it in time. The man who had been leaning against the wall, his back to her, had turned around and now faced her.

She raised a finger to her lips and said, "Shhh."

Then she started walking toward him. He yanked an arm back and whipped out a gun. Before he could bear down on her, she shot him in the right shoulder, knocking the gun away in a wide arc. The gun landed a dozen feet from him in the next aisle. He grabbed for his wound as he slipped to his knees, a loud grunt emanating from his lips.

"What the fuck was that?" Deep Voice shouted.

Sarah ran to close the distance and stopped at the corner, gun in one hand, broom in the other. Three men flanked another man suspended by his feet, blood coloring them red.

She looked closer at the man on his back, his feet in the air. His face seemed familiar for some reason.

Holy shit!

The random man on the street she had forced to send the text. Was this her fault? Is that why she was supposed to send the text and then stop the torture?

What the hell's going on, Vivian?

The wounded guy behind her was crawling to the next aisle. He was probably in search of his weapon. Sarah stepped back from the edge of the row, grabbed the man's shirt, spun him toward the open area, and then shoved him.

The others opened fire as their comrade fell face down. Bullets ricocheted off the floor, some of them hitting the wounded man.

"Stop fucking shooting," Deep Voice hollered.

The noise stopped.

"Step out of hiding and identify yourself," Deep Voice said.

"I've got the broom," Sarah shouted back.

She swung her arm out, tossed it toward them, and then jumped back. It clanged down and rolled away, no one making a move for it.

"A woman, eh? Okay, here's the deal, bitch. Come out so we can talk, or I'll put a bullet in Mark here. Don't test me. Hey, Mark, you want a little metal in the forehead courtesy of our new guest?"

"Come on, man," the guy on the ground pleaded.

Vivian's message to stop the torture probably didn't mean stopping it by getting the guy killed. Although as much as that would stop it, Sarah was sure she was supposed to walk out of the building with the guy still alive.

"Three seconds," Deep Voice shouted.

"Shit," Sarah said under her breath. "Now what?"

"Okay, say goodbye to Mark."

Sarah decided to move into the open just as a gun fired.

Chapter 11

Bruce jumped in his unmarked cruiser and hit the lights. On Las Vegas Boulevard, he made a U-turn and headed east toward the trailer park.

He couldn't believe his brother was involved in any way with the criminal element of Vegas. There had to be an explanation. His ID had shown up at a murder scene. Jake hadn't called ahead to let his brother know he would be in town, which he always did in the past. That left Bruce with an uneasy feeling. It meant Jake was in Vegas for something he wanted Bruce to have no knowledge of.

If it weren't for Russell Anderson coming into the station earlier that night, Bruce would've had no idea his brother was there until homicide called. He wouldn't have been able to track him to the New York, New York Hotel, which was where he always stayed because they comped him a room. Jake even had his own casino host.

If Jake was in trouble, then what could it be? And why not let his big brother in on it so he could help?

Bruce hit the gas harder and ran a red light, the siren warning people to stay out of his way. The streets had thinned as the hour wore on past midnight, allowing Bruce to navigate quicker.

He jumped when his phone rang beside him.

Private caller.

He picked it up. "Yeah?"

"Say goodbye to your brother Jake."

"Who's this?"

"Russell Anderson."

"What're you talking about? You threatening my brother?"

"No. But he won't live through the night if you don't listen to Sarah. I told you about that."

Russell sounded like he was crying.

"Just tell me what's going on," Bruce said, slowing the speed of his vehicle a bit. He didn't want to race down the Las Vegas strip at seventy miles an hour while on the phone. Too many things could go wrong.

"Sarah's in trouble and needs your help. She's entering a warehouse in the west end right now. There are guns. People are going to be shot. Believe me. Hurry, or your family will pay a large price."

"You want me to go to this warehouse and save Sarah Roberts and then listen to her?"

"Yes."

Russell was definitely crying.

Crime scene or warehouse. Job or family or family and job. Bruce decided to go out on a limb. Russell had come through in unique ways before, and Bruce trusted Russell's letters. If he were to trust Russell, now would be the best time. If he was wrong, he could pick Russell up, grab his brother and talk this thing out. Tyrone Percy would still be dead.

"Fine, where is it? Where am I going?"

Russell told him. Bruce made another U-turn and headed west.

"What am I to expect when I arrive at this warehouse?"

He didn't receive an answer. Russell had already hung up.

"Shit." He smacked the steering wheel.

Then he dialed Detective Mackey back.

"Mackey here."

"Look, I can't come right away. I've been delayed for a bit."

"You want me to put a call out on the street for officers to pick up your brother?"

"No, wait for me. I'll be there shortly. Something else came up that I personally have to tend to."

"Something else came up that's more important than family?"

"Yes and no. It is family, but …"

"Your brother's ID was found at a murder scene. Where would finding an ID like this normally lead a homicide detective? So, Bruce, tell me, what do you want me to do? My call to you was a professional courtesy."

"Listen, my brother didn't do anything wrong. I'm on my way to meet someone who might know more about this. Also, I know where Jake is, and my partner has his hotel under surveillance. Everything's under control on my end. I will bring Jake in. I just can't come out to the trailer park right now. As soon as I finish what I have to do and grab

Jake, I'll bring him in. You'll see us within a few hours, sometime before dawn."

"Fine, have it your way. I'll see you at the station before dawn. Just make sure you're there, and Jake is with you."

The phone clicked off.

Bruce tossed it in the seat beside him.

"Fuck," he yelled and smacked the steering wheel twice.

Then he turned off the strip and headed west toward the warehouse along the back roads.

Chapter 12

THE GUN THAT FIRED wasn't the one in the hand of the man with the deep voice. He was down on his knees, trying to hold the blood in his chest as it gurgled out of an open wound. The other two men spun frantically, their weapons raised, trying to ascertain where the threat was coming from.

From where Sarah was, she couldn't see who had shot Deep Voice, but whoever it was, she now had an ally.

She wiped the sweat from her eyes, blinked a couple of times, and peeked around the edge of the aisle.

"We have you surrounded," she shouted at the two men, still trying to find a target. "Set your guns on the ground and kick them away from you."

The men looked at each other. They stood in the open. Their boss was on the ground, bleeding to death. It was obvious who had the upper hand. Each one set their weapons down, then raised their hands above their heads.

"Kick them away," Sarah shouted.

Both kicked their guns away at the same time without

lowering their hands.

Sarah stepped out from behind the row and started toward them, keeping an eye on the area where she assumed the gunman was.

Halfway across the distance, a sudden movement from Deep Voice pulled her attention to him as he pulled his arm up fast. A shiny metal piece appeared out of thin air.

Sarah dove for the ground. His gun fired twice, both bullets whizzing so close she heard them cut the air by her head.

After smacking the ground on her right shoulder, she twisted toward him and pulled her trigger. The one bullet that exited her barrel hit Deep Voice in his left eye. His head rocked back, blood shooting up in an arc over his head. Then he was laid out on his back and didn't move again.

In the commotion, the other two men had jumped at the chance to reclaim their weapons. The first man lifted his to aim at Sarah, but she already had a bead on him.

On reflex, borne of years of dealing with these kinds of people, she aimed high at his chest and hit the side of his throat. Then she turned slightly for the other guy, but he was running behind a row of fabric and was lost to sight.

A gun fired from that direction.

Sarah got to her feet. "Identify yourself," she shouted. "Who's there?"

The warehouse was quiet except for the groans of the tortured man still suspended by his feet.

He was still alive. The torture had been stopped.

She moved to the side and stood by the end of a row. Without knowing who else was in the warehouse, she had to remain cautious even if they felt like an ally. She silently moved to the corner, paused, brought her weapon down, and peeked around the edge.

The third man was flat out on the floor, blood circling his abdomen. Down the length of the aisle, a man stood by the door where she had entered the warehouse earlier. The light from an outside security lamp illuminated his face enough for her to see the scar.

It was the man who had warned her to not send the text. The man she had chased by Bellagio, who had cried when he asked her not to do it.

A police siren blared in the distance, signaling they would be on-site at any moment.

"Hey," Sarah yelled at him. "Who are you?"

He stared at her from the door without responding.

"Why are you following me? Do I know you?"

The man turned and stepped through the door. Sarah broke into a run down the length of the aisle to the door.

Outside, the man was gone.

Headlights turned into the driveway, a red flashing light from the dash of the car. Sarah looked down at the gun in her hand. It was registered to her, but she didn't want it taken away.

She jumped back into the warehouse as the police car halted outside. One row up, she stashed it between two large rolls of fabric. It couldn't be seen. Without moving the large rows with a machine of some kind, no one would find her weapon.

Then she got on her knees and placed her hands behind her head.

"Police," a man shouted. "We're coming in."

A lone man entered through the door. He saw Sarah and

aimed his weapon at her.

"Are you Sarah Roberts?" he asked, the emotion in his voice cracking it.

"Who wants to know?" she asked.

"I'm Detective Bruce Collins."

"Then yeah, I'm Sarah."

"What's the message you have for me?"

"Huh?"

"The message. Aren't you supposed to tell me something about my brother?"

"I have no idea what you're talking about."

"Are you armed?"

"No."

"What happened here?" Collins asked as he lowered his weapon slightly. "Is there anyone else here?"

"Can I put my hands down?"

"Not yet." He ran over to her. "Stand up."

She did.

"Turn and lean onto that roll of fabric."

"Not until I see some ID," Sarah said. "I'm not turning my back on you until I know you're a cop."

He fished out his ID, which Sarah inspected. Then she nodded and turned around, placing her hands high on the roll of fabric.

He frisked her but avoided going into the pockets of her pants.

"Is there anything in those pockets I need to worry about?" he asked.

"Can I turn around?"

"Yes."

She did and then flipped out her pockets. "I'm clean."

The detective holstered his weapon. "What happened here?"

"There are four men. Three of them are either wounded or dead."

The detective brought this weapon up again. Sarah raised her hands.

"Hey, take it easy. The area's secure."

"What happened? Did you shoot these men?"

"I walked in that door and discovered three men torturing a guy back there."

"Show me."

Sarah turned to walk to the back. Detective Collins would be able to see the man at the end of the row. She moved to the other side of the torture area so Collins could see the entire thing with her still in his sights.

"Holy shit," he muttered. "What the fuck is this?"

"My thoughts exactly."

"You did this?" Collins asked.

"Did what? Torture the guy? No. Stop the torture? Yes. Well, with a little help."

"Help?" Collins looked completely confused.

"Yeah, some guy with a scar on his face came in at the right moment—"

Collins glared at her. "A scar?"

"That's what I said."

"Russell Anderson."

"Sorry, didn't get his name. He was in, then out. You know this guy?"

Collins nodded.

He pulled out a cell phone and called the crime scene in.

"What happened?" Collins asked.

"I showed up. They were torturing this guy." She had to figure out how to give her statement without revealing she used her own gun. Ballistics would figure it out later, but she would be long gone by then. "When I asked them to stop, this one," she pointed at the guy with the deep voice, "said he was going to shoot that guy." She pointed at the man with his feet suspended in shackles. "The man with the facial scar showed up out of nowhere and shot him." She pointed at Deep Voice again. "Then those two wanted to shoot me. The man with the scar helped out there, too. This scar guy is an enigma. It's the third time I've seen him tonight."

"The man with the scar." Bruce was shaking his head. "You're saying he was here, and he shot these men?"

"Yes, that's what I'm saying. But he did it in self-defense. Actually, third-party self-defense."

Collins mumbled something.

"What's that? You have a history with Scar Man?"

"Doesn't concern you. Why are you here in the first place?"

More sirens blared outside.

"Long story."

"We've got time."

"It's all her fault," the man suspended by his ankles broke his silence. "Keep her away from me."

His feet were covered in blood. Slash marks from a whip covered his naked body. He seemed to be waking from a pain-filled stupor as he stared at Sarah, his eyes wide with fear and pain.

"Keep her away from me," he shouted again, his voice echoing in the cavernous warehouse.

"Take it easy," Sarah said. She backed away from the guy

to calm him down a little.

"Step aside," Collins said. "Now, get back down on your knees."

"What?" Sarah asked. "Why?"

"Just do it." The cop's gun came back up.

"I fucking hate this part."

"What's that?"

"I did nothing wrong. I stopped these assholes from torturing him. Why you gotta piss on me?"

"I have three men shot in a warehouse. I have a man tied up saying it's all your fault. I think it's reasonable that I take you downtown and at least get your statement. That's the minimum. Or I arrest you for murder right now, and we'll let the courts figure it all out."

"I just wish I wasn't late for the torture. Next time I won't be late, and then everything will work out."

Collins was moving closer, as were the sirens outside.

"Late for what?" he asked. Handcuffs came out of the back of his pants.

"You're kidding, right? I'll go willingly."

"Hands on your head. Do it now."

"Oh, for fuck's sake. Listen, I stopped the torture. I'm the good one here."

"Tell that to the judge." Collins smacked the cuffs on so hard she winced.

The naked man mumbled something.

"What was that?" Collins asked as he slipped his weapon away.

"They said they were going to violate me with that broom there," the man said. Sarah watched Collins's eyes as he saw the broom. "When I woke earlier, she tossed the broom over here."

Collins glanced over his shoulder at her. "Stories don't exactly match, do they? Interesting."

"Fuck your interesting."

"Doesn't help your case." He looked down at the bleeding man on his back as officers filed in the side door of the warehouse.

"Back here," Collins yelled to them.

"I saw her earlier tonight," the naked man said. "She pulled a gun on me and made me text a message to someone. That's why I'm here. All because of her. This whole thing is her fault."

Collins snuck another look her way.

"Fuckin' shit," Sarah mumbled. "That's what this is."

Vivian, what gives? None of this makes sense.

"I can't believe Tyrone is dead," the naked guy said as he started to cry.

"Tyrone Percy?" Collins asked.

"Yeah, you know him?"

Officers moved into the area, two of them stepping in behind Sarah. No one said anything as they all listened to Collins talk to the naked man. Paramedics entered through the side door with a stretcher.

"Homicide discovered his body," Collins said.

"In his trailer?"

Collins nodded. "Yeah. What do you know about it?"

"He killed him." Naked man pointed at Deep Voice. "Told me about it."

"See," Sarah said. "I did you a favor, asshole."

"Shut up," Collins shouted at her.

"Some of his men were headed somewhere to pick up the

guy who texted me back …”

Sarah stopped listening. Back on the Las Vegas Strip, when she made him text the message, she also made him erase the text but didn’t consider the man would text him back.

“That’s it,” Sarah said.

“I thought I told you to shut up,” Collins shouted and turned around to face her.

“Four men left earlier. They were headed to see the man who texted him back.” She nodded at the naked man. “I know where they were headed, and now I know why your name sounded familiar.”

Collins moved away from the naked man and walked over to Sarah. “What’s that about my name?”

“Uncuff me, and we’ll talk about it.”

“Fuck you. Tell me what I want to know.”

“Fuck you back.” She looked at the floor, knowing she held the power again.

Collins placed his weapon against the skin of her forehead, pushing her head back. One of the officers on the side touched his arm and asked Collins what the hell he was doing.

“Tell me what you know.”

“Take your weapon out of my face,” Sarah whispered. “Do not point that thing at me unless you intend to use it.” She gritted her teeth. “This will only end badly for you if you go against me.”

“You threatening a police officer?” Collins asked.

“You want to hear about Jake or not?” Sarah said. “I’m assuming he’s your brother.”

Collins pulled the weapon away from her and holstered

it.

"I want her in the back of my cruiser, now. She goes downtown with me. No more bullshit from this one."

Rough hands guided her outside. One of the men opened the back of a cruiser and shoved her inside by the top of her head.

After a thirty-second wait, Collins came outside and headed for the car. He jumped in the front seat and turned to face her.

"Tell me about Jake."

"Cuffs off first."

He tossed the keys in the back. She turned in her seat, grabbed them by feel, and began working the little key into the hole of the first cuff. In under ten seconds, she was uncuffed and rubbing her wrists.

"Start driving."

He turned on the car. "Where're we going?"

"The New York, New York Hotel."

"I should have fucking known it," Collins said and hit the gas.

Chapter 13

Bruce called Munro on the way to the New York Hotel to let her know he was coming back and had Sarah Roberts. He warned her about the men who were probably on their way, too. They would have a ten- to fifteen-minute head start, which meant they would probably be there at any moment.

"That's four men who were instructed to hospitalize Jake," Bruce said. "Got it?"

"Yes. Got it."

"Have you seen Jake yet?"

"No. Nothing. He's probably too afraid to come back down knowing you're looking for him. He saw you by the elevator. No doubt about it."

"Okay, give me ten minutes. I'll be there. In the meantime, can you call that judge, Mallory, the one that likes us? Tell him we have an emergency and all we need is the New York Hotel to give us the room number of my brother. We have reason to believe he's in danger."

"Already did that."

"Really?"

"Right after you left. What, you thought I would just sit here and stare at elevators? Too boring. I've been on the phone non-stop since you left me here."

"You're the best. I knew there was a reason you're my partner."

"Just get here," Munro said.

Bruce tossed the phone on the seat beside him and looked at Sarah in the mirror.

"So, what's your story?"

"Don't have one," she said.

"Sure you do. Everybody's got a story."

"Not this girl."

"Why are you in Vegas, then? Tell me that."

"You wouldn't believe me if I told you."

"Try me."

Sarah met his eyes in the mirror. "My dead sister told me to come here and stop that torture at the warehouse. I was sent to save that dick who tried to say I was helping those other assholes. The thanks I get." She shook her head.

"Your dead sister?"

"Yup."

"Your dead sister?" he repeated.

Sarah's eyes narrowed. For a moment, he thought she was going to attack him.

"You know who I am, don't you?"

"Yeah, I know your name. Some of your exploits, too. You're in the papers now and then. I remember the FLDS compound bust-up. Haven't you been in Europe and then Canada for some time?"

"Why the fuck were you giving me shit back there at the

warehouse then? If you know who I am, that we're on the same side, why fuck with me?"

"You always swear this much?"

"Now you're my dad? Gonna wash my mouth out?"

"You want to answer my question?"

"It's just a sound. Lighten up. Would you rather I say *darn you* to the bad guys? Doesn't wash in my world. I've seen too many people die, get shot, watched teenage girls being trafficked for sex at that FLDS compound, and had to kill more people than I ever wanted to. So I don't worry about a fucking word. Get a life. Get over it. Grow up. It's just a sound."

"Okay, okay, I get it. So why stop that torture?" he asked. A red light was coming up. He slowed, made sure it was clear, then raced through and turned into the hotel entrance.

"Probably because my sister made me send that text. After that, the guy's getting tortured. Leads me to believe it's connected."

Her voice had taken on an are-you-stupid tone. He hated to be patronized. His ego was taking a hit, too. He was a cop. That usually garnered a little respect, but evidently, the only thing this girl respected was the survival of the fittest. In her world, it was every man—or woman—for themselves, and everyone was an equal, badge or no badge.

He parked on the curb where people were queueing at a taxi stand. A valet came over. Bruce waved him off and spun around, an arm on the back of the seat.

"Can I trust you to sit here quietly while I go in and get my brother, Jake?"

"No."

"What do you mean, no?"

"I won't be here when you come out."

"I could arrest you. We'll have a huge investigation into what happened at the warehouse, and finally, a judge will decide your fate. Or you could sit here quietly, and when I come back, we figure everything out quietly."

"I'll be long gone by the time you come back out. My time in Vegas is over."

He flipped his hands in the air. "What the hell do you want then?"

"I go in with you. I got a glimpse of the four men sent here to harm your brother. I can help. If you know my name, you know this is my area of expertise. You will also know that cop cars never contain me. In fact, they're the most popular vehicle I steal."

He thought about it for a moment. "Okay, you can come in. But will you stick around long enough for me to get the whole story from Jake and Russell Anderson?"

"Who's Russell Anderson?"

"The man with the scar. His name is Russell Anderson."

"Yeah, I'll stick around. I want to learn more about this Russell Anderson. He's been following me all night, and I want to thank him for helping me out at the warehouse."

"Good. Sounds like we each have something the other wants. When my brother is safe, we sit, have coffee, and figure everything out. Deal?"

"Deal."

He turned to get out of the car, then stopped and looked at her in the mirror. "I get from you that you keep your word. Is my intuition correct?"

"I never lie or bluff. If you can't keep your word, then what the hell good are you?"

He nodded, got out, and opened her door. Sarah got out and fiddled with the back of her pants.

"Everything okay?"

"Yeah. Let's go."

They entered the casino and headed for Munro. He spied her at the corner of the bar.

"This Sarah?" Munro asked.

Bruce nodded.

Munro looked her up and down. "You're *the* Sarah Roberts?"

"What's this?" Sarah asked. "I thought we were coming to stop your brother from being put into the ICU?"

"Yeah," Munro said. "You're Sarah Roberts. I can tell. Let's go."

"You got the room number?" Bruce asked.

"One minute ago," she said as she led the way to the elevators. "That bitch Rose from behind the counter wouldn't budge, even after a courtesy call from the judge. Her clerk slipped it into my hand on her lunch break."

"Good to hear."

Munro pushed the up button and turned to size up Sarah. Bruce thought it funny how women had to do that.

"I'm not a lesbian," Sarah said.

Bruce smiled for the first time in hours.

"Why would you say that?" Munro asked.

"The way you're staring at me. You're either rude and don't know social boundaries, or you're interested in getting me into bed. I just thought I'd be clear at the get-go that I have no problem with your lifestyle, I'm just not down for the carpet."

"Holy shit," Munro said. "You are a piece of work."

The elevator dinged. The door opened. At least ten people exited, heading for the tables, some already quite drunk. The trio stepped on. Munro hit the buttons, and they began to ascend.

"I would think with your profile you wouldn't offend that easy," Munro said.

"I'm not offended. I just wanted to be clear so you don't get your hopes up and then get disappointed. And I don't have a profile. You can't profile what no one understands."

Munro whistled. "What would Freud have made of you?"

"He would've debated it with Jung, who would have tried to sleep with me, and in the end, they would've both been disappointed and never filed a paper in any psychiatric journal because nothing would be conclusive. I would probably end up in an asylum in those days. But then I would break out, and no one would hear from me again."

The elevator slowed.

"Okay, ladies, enough with the bickering."

"Oh, we're not bickering," Munro said. "We're just getting acquainted."

The door opened. Bruce motioned for the two women to stay back. With his other hand on the butt of his weapon, he edged out and peeked into the hallway. After he saw it was clear, he motioned for them to follow him.

The hallway twisted to the left and to the right on each side. The hotel's design was unique to match the outside, which was built to resemble multiple buildings in downtown New York.

Munro pointed to the right and whispered Jake's room number to Bruce. The detectives took the lead, with Sarah following close behind. After two turns in the corridor, there was an open stretch. Midway down, he thought he heard a grunt of some kind from up ahead. He stopped them with a raised hand.

The noise came again.

He started running, watching the room numbers as they raced by. Three doors down, two doors. He slowed as he came upon his brother's room.

Another grunt sounded from behind the door. He placed an ear close to the door to try to figure out how many were inside.

"Where's the money, asshole?" someone asked.

"I told you, I gave it to the girl." Jake's voice. "All of it."

Another voice joined in. "I can't find his wallet anywhere."

"I told you," Jake shouted. "She fucking stole my wallet. Pickpocketed me."

Someone got slapped.

"My boss told me to come here looking for money, and we can't leave until we get some. Or you get a free ride in an ambulance and a week's stay in the ICU."

Bruce had heard enough. He motioned for the two women to step back. Then he brought his gun around to aim at the doorknob. In case someone was near the door, he ensured his aim went sideways. Once the bullet entered the room, it would go into the wall by the door and possibly the bathroom.

He pulled the trigger twice, fast and hard.

The second the bullets left the barrel, he stepped back and then charged the door. His shoulder bounced it open easily, but he lost his balance and fell. When he landed, he spun around to take the room in, his gun up and ready to continue firing if he needed to.

Munro stepped over him and moved farther inside.

That's what partners are for, he thought.

No one moved. There were three men standing around his brother, who sat in the chair by the desk. Blood trickled from his brother's mouth, and it looked like he had a fat lip already growing.

"I was wondering when you would get here," Jake said.

Bruce got to his feet while Munro covered the three perps.

"This him?" Munro asked.

"Yeah," Bruce said. "How's it going, Bro?"

"We were having a nice chat until you rudely interrupted us," Jake said, a smile playing across his lips.

"Sorry about that. How come I always have to rescue you from bullies? Since we were kids and you were beaten up in the schoolyard, I've had to break it up. Getting tired of that, Jake."

"You think you could read these idiots their rights?" Jake asked.

"I'll do one better."

The one closest to Jake looked worried. The other two looked too stupid to be worried. One had a scowl on his face and the other a blank stare.

People would come into the hallway to see what that noise was when he shot the door handle. The commotion was less than a minute away.

"The big guy with the deep voice back at the linen warehouse ..." Bruce saw recognition in their eyes. "He's dead. The other two who were left behind at the fabric warehouse are dead, too. The guy you were torturing, well, he's fine. I know because I was just there. Now, on the floor slowly and place your hands on the back of your heads. You're all under arrest. I'm a Las Vegas police officer bound by the confines of my badge, after all. That means any sudden movement will scare me, and you could join your friends in the dirt motel. Get down or go down."

Something clicked behind him. It sounded like a gun.

Then he remembered. Sarah had said *four* men came to hurt Jake.

Shit.

He turned around slowly. The fourth man stood a foot away, his gun one inch from the tip of Bruce's ear.

"Drop the gun, fucking pig."

In a blur of movement, someone rammed into the fourth guy's arm, knocking it in the air so fast that the arm snapped at the elbow. The gun he had been holding flipped harmlessly across the room, landing by the door to the next room.

Sarah Roberts shoved the guy to the floor.

"The man said, either get down or go down." She looked at Bruce and then at the others in the room. "That's one down. Who's next?"

Blessed Sarah.

The man at her feet howled and stared at his elbow where a tiny bit of white bone stuck out of his flesh.

Sarah lifted her leg high like she wanted to step on a large spider and drove it down into the guy's right shoulder, laying him out flat.

She landed on him, handcuffs snapping over the wrist of the unbroken arm, the other cuff slapping onto the leg of the heavy desk.

"Pointing a gun at an officer of the law," Sarah said as

she looked at the man below her, shaking her head, "while he is trying to perform his sworn duties will get you fucked up every time."

Munro had kept the trio by Jake covered with her weapon. Bruce faced Sarah.

"The cuffs …" he said and then got it. "Those were the ones I put on you and then tossed the keys to you."

She smiled.

"You stole my cuffs."

"There a problem with that, Officer?" she asked.

"No, no, I just wanted to thank you."

"Then thank me."

He nodded and smiled back. She was impressive.

"Thank you, Sarah."

He turned back to the trio. "Let's go, on the ground. All of you."

The men got down without any more convincing and were secured quickly. Munro called for backup as Bruce handled hotel security.

Jake wanted to explain his side of the story, but Bruce told him to wait until they got to the station. There would be lots of time to talk.

***

An hour later, Detectives Collins and Munro sat in the front seat of their cruiser with Jake and Sarah in the back as Bruce drove them to the police station.

They entered the building through a side door. Bruce led them all to a conference room. Sarah expected an interrogation room. Maybe Bruce wanted it less intimidating since Jake was family.

Once settled, Munro grabbed four coffees while Bruce stepped out to take a call. She put on another pot and brought a box of leftover donuts from the lunch room.

"Whose are those?" Bruce asked as he reentered the room.

"No idea," Munro said between mouthfuls. "I just grabbed them. We have to eat something."

Sarah took a pass on the donuts. On her second coffee, she started the meeting by telling them who she was and what she did.

"Whether you believe in what I do or not, that's how it is. One of my closest friends is a cop. His name is Parkman. He's in Santa Rosa with my parents, last I heard. Call him. He'll verify who I am."

She went on to say that she was supposed to text the message Jake had received.

Jake piped in to explain that he got the text and thought it was the girl he was supposed to meet.

"What girl?" Bruce asked. "The one who stole your wallet?"

"Yeah, how'd you know about that?"

"I heard you say it through the door at the hotel. Also, your wallet turned up at a murder scene earlier tonight."

"What?" Jake's face paled. After a moment, he rested his head on the table. "What have I gotten myself into?"

"Look, whatever has happened tonight, Munro and I saw you enter that elevator. Then Munro staked the elevator banks out until we broke into your room. I'm sure once they establish a time of death, the investigators will use us as your alibi."

Jake kept his head down.

"Also, the call I just took," Bruce continued, "was from homicide. The girl who found her boyfriend dead was the girl who took the ten thousand from you."

That got Jake's head back up.

"She confessed to the whole scam."

"She did? It was a scam?" Jake asked.

"Yeah. She told the homicide detectives that she felt Tyrone's murder was punishment for going after you. Karma or something. Who knows? The good thing is, she's not pregnant and never was, according to homicide. She only did this scam because she got you to think you slept with her, which according to her statement, you didn't. After I told them where you were all night and that I'm talking to you here in the station, homicide told me on the phone that you're guilty of being an idiot, that's all."

"Oh, shit, okay, I can take that. What a relief. I had no idea."

"No idea? About what? Whether you cheated on your wife or not? You don't know if you had sex? Who does that?"

"I was drunk. It was a huge party. I passed out. When I woke up, she was beside me and told me I was awesome the night before. I ran out of there and tried to forget the whole thing. Last week, I got a call and a demand for money to get an abortion. Then yesterday, she wanted forty thousand more. I had no idea what I was going to do."

"Just be happy that's all over," Bruce said.

"Should have listened to the text I sent you," Sarah added. "That's what my sister does. She tried to save you."

"Why use the tortured guy?" Munro asked.

"To get me there, to meet Bruce, and to convince Bruce

to come and save Jake. The way things are sitting right now, I can see how it all ties in, but I never see the whole picture at the beginning. That's Vivian's job. All the bad guys are dealt with, and all the good guys are safe."

"Wrong," Munro said. "You're forgetting the tortured guy. He's in the hospital, and it doesn't look like he'll walk again for a few months. And who killed the scammer's boyfriend, Tyrone Percy? Seems to me we're just getting started."

Sarah tapped the table. "That's for the police to handle. If Vivian lets me in on something, then I'll handle it. If she doesn't, I'm out of here."

That reminded her that her bike was a block from the warehouse in the west end, and her gun was stuck inside on one of the racks between two fabric rolls. She'd grab her bike but probably have to leave the gun behind. Buying another one would be a bitch, but shit happens.

"Stick around for a few days," Bruce said. "We may have more questions, and I'll need a full statement from you before you go."

Sarah nodded.

"There was one more thing I wanted to ask you about," Bruce said as he got up and paced, coffee cup in hand. "When I showed up at the warehouse, you said something about the man with the scar." Munro shot him a glance. "What was that again?"

"Earlier, you called him Russell Anderson."

Bruce nodded. Munro turned her gaze to Sarah.

"He's been following me. He showed up at the warehouse. That's all I know." She waited a heartbeat, then added. "You know him better than me."

The two detectives exchanged a glance.

Bruce turned back to Sarah. "We know him well, but he lives a relatively quiet life. Frankly, I'm surprised he showed up tonight. Fighting crime isn't his style."

"What is?" Sarah asked. "*Not* fighting crime?"

They exchanged another glance. She was onto something. This Russell Anderson was an enigma. She needed to find him. She needed to learn how he knew about her and what business he had with her.

But that would have to wait. Once the police let her go, she would get her bike, find a motel, sleep the day away, and then go find Russell Anderson.

She wondered if he was like her. Did someone from the other side speak to him? The last time she met someone like her, he tried to kill her.

If that was the case this time, why help her at the warehouse?

The answers she needed meant she would be staying in Vegas longer than she wanted.

Chapter 14

BY THE TIME THEY let Sarah go, the sun was up, her nerves were shot from answering the same questions over and over, and her head ached from lack of sleep, too much coffee, or both.

She didn't consider asking for a ride back to her bike. All she wanted was a hotel room, a bed, and food. She would take a cab to get her bike later in the day or that night.

She started down the street, watching to see if Russell was following her again. She couldn't see anyone. Not even the cops.

She didn't think to grab her sunglasses out of the bag on her bike. When she parked it late last night, she thought she would stop a torture and grab a motel room. Wandering the streets of Vegas the next day, far from her bike, seemed unlikely the previous night.

The air was already thick and hot. Within a block of the police station, she broke into a sweat, and her head doubled its pounding.

A block up Martin Luther King Boulevard, she could either go left, which would take her under the freeway bridge toward Las Vegas Boulevard, or go right and enter the large hospital where she would find a pharmacy. Painkillers would be in a pharmacy.

She decided on left, walked under the bridge, and kept going until she hit the strip—Las Vegas Boulevard. At any time, she could grab a cab, but it felt good to walk. She had nothing to do, nowhere to go, and no messages from Vivian. She wanted a motel and a bed, but walking off the headache would work for now.

She checked her phone. No messages.

Across the street was a large drugstore. She took that as a message to kill the headache.

She crossed at the light and entered the drug store, a loud bell announcing her arrival. The pain in her head made her squint at the sound of the bell and the bright lights in the store. A short, older woman with white hair stood behind the counter. She smiled when Sarah entered.

"Headache," Sarah said. "Painkillers?"

"Down aisle two," the woman responded.

Her voice saddened Sarah. It reminded her of Esmerelda. Then she thought of Dolan and tried to push them from her thoughts mentally. Two good people, taken too early.

In the painkiller section, she examined the small boxes for pill strength.

The front doorbell sounded as someone else entered. Sarah saw the profile of the woman behind the counter as she greeted the new customer. She looked away and chose the 400mg pill bottle. She could take three or four of them to knock the shit out of her headache and let her sleep like a log.

Fatigue could be a nasty bitch.

She walked along the aisle. The woman behind the counter backed up and bumped into the display behind her, fear evident on her face now.

A man stepped into view with a shotgun.

"For fuck's sake," Sarah mumbled. "You're kidding me."

Sarah flattened herself against the side of the aisle. Her elbow struck a small box of tablets. It rocked on the shelf, teetered to the edge, and fell. She caught it before it could clatter on the floor, then exhaled slowly, calming her nerves.

The aisle was too long for her to make it to the end undetected. Twenty feet from her sat a small square wire display container filled with bouncy balls. Crouched down on her knees, she might be able to remain concealed there. If this were a fast smash-and-grab, the guy with the gun would be in and out. No need to hide for any length of time. Anything longer than that, the people in the store were in trouble.

An image of her gun stashed between fabric rolls at the warehouse on the west side of Vegas flashed into her mind.

Great.

"Move, woman," the man ordered.

The clerk stepped from behind the counter. The punk grabbed her shirt and dragged her out of Sarah's view.

"What're you doing?" the clerk shouted.

"Shut up, bitch."

The clerk grunted from an aisle over as she was smacked hard.

Sarah had to do something. But he had a gun, and she didn't. A robbery in broad daylight, walking distance from the police station, was brazen. They had to be high on something.

"I got the front covered," another man yelled. "The door's locked."

A deeper voice shouted, "I got the back."

A man appeared at the entrance to her aisle and scanned the length of it. His eyes stopped on her. He brought his weapon up and aimed it at her like he was hunting game. He held it high, his eye peering through the sights.

"We got a customer here," he yelled. "She was trying to escape. Should I just shoot her?"

Two male voices responded. One told him to kill her. Shoot her in the face. The other said to keep her as a prisoner.

Sarah couldn't control the full-body shake that took over. Lack of sleep, proper food, and all that she had been through since arriving in Vegas was taking its toll. And she was unarmed.

The punk moved closer, his gun jostling in his hands.

She still had the bottle of painkillers she'd wanted to buy in one hand and the small box that she caught in the other. As the man approached, she released both boxes and let them fall harmlessly at her feet.

He didn't wear a mask, which wasn't good. At least twenty-two, Caucasian, and he spoke with an accent. Sounded Cuban. Tattoos on his arms, with a long one rising out of his shirt that covered the right side of his neck. He snorted hard like he had a cold. The sign of too much cocaine.

When he was four feet from her, he stopped.

"On your knees, bitch."

"Are you sure you want—"

"Now!" he shouted.

The gun shook in his hands when he yelled. She worried the weapon would fire by mistake.

"Okay," she whispered. "Take it easy."

She kept her hands visible and slowly got to her knees.

"Goodbye, whore."

Then he pulled the trigger.

Chapter 15

Russell Anderson climbed out of the large box in the back
of the pharmacy. He stretched and twisted his shoulders left
and right to loosen up after being in the box for an hour. Then
he flicked his hair out of his face, licked his palm, and
slicked his hair back, trying to keep it restrained.

The clock on the wall said he had three minutes to get
into place. He didn't want to do this, but Sarah had forced
him to. If only she hadn't come to Vegas. Now people were
dead, and she was in danger. Whether things worked out or
not, it upset him to be so involved, but this was what fate did.
It served only cold dishes.

This wasn't how he worked. He sent pictures and letters
to the police so they could do their job. It wasn't his job to
fight crime, and he resented the fact that he had to be
involved again.

But family came first. After losing his daughter, he
would rather die than let more of his family suffer needlessly.

He grabbed a metal bar and got in position behind the

doors leading to the store's front.

"Shoot her in the face," someone shouted.

"Keep her as a hostage," another voice called out.

He checked the clock. Feet scuffled on the other side of the door.

A loud boom sounded from the front of the store as someone fired a weapon. A woman screamed. Then another. He couldn't tell how many.

But his job was to wait. Everything would work out if he waited.

With Penny gone from his life, he didn't care if he died. That would be a blessing. In fact, on many levels, he was already dead. No one knew his name anymore. He didn't speak it. He had no friends and existed daily on the charity of rich strangers who traveled to Vegas hoping to hit a large jackpot.

He kept his digital camera hidden when begging for money. When not begging, he took the pictures he was supposed to take. Then mailed them to Detective Collins. One of the reasons he stayed in Vegas was his father. As far as Penny was concerned, Russell's father lived in Las Vegas, and Russell was set to meet him soon.

It was probably what kept him alive. The pictures he provided to the police offered him a purpose and a way to give back after what had happened to his daughter. If he died, he would be content that he gave something back in the time he had left, and he would welcome the end of his existence on earth.

Seeing Penny again was all he needed to heal his soul, and giving his soul to the Higher Power above was the only way to see her.

The clock counted down the seconds.

Four …

Three …

He tightened his grip on the metal bar.

Two …

One …

The door beside him banged open. A young man walked through, a long-barreled handgun in his grip raised and ready to fire. The man fanned the weapon's tip right and then started to the left.

The door swung shut behind him.

Russell brought the bar up high and swung it down toward the back of the man's skull.

It connected with a solid crack. The man's knees gave out, and he fell to the stockroom floor like a sack of dirt.

Chapter 16

SARAH OPENED HER EYES. She breathed in deeply after holding her breath for a few seconds.

The gun had fired so close that her ears still rang. Beside her, a pile of destroyed pill boxes and containers littered the floor.

Either the idiot had shot into the display rack by accident, or he had done it to scare her. Whatever the reason, she was certainly afraid, which angered her. Trigger-happy idiots with guns almost always meant someone would end up dead or in the hospital.

She kept her hands visible and her body in the open. If she saw an opportunity, she would take it. There was a high chance she would be shot and killed if she didn't try something.

Vivian hadn't warned her, which meant Sarah wasn't prepared. No weapon and no idea what they wanted.

He was saying something about moving down the aisle toward the back, but she couldn't hear him clearly yet. She turned and started walking, her mind going over options.

Then it occurred to her that the headache was completely gone. Vivian probably had something to do with that. If giving her the headache was meant to get Sarah inside the pharmacy during a robbery, why not just tell her with another message? That way, she could've been better prepared.

Or perhaps having a weapon would've gotten her shot.

Since it was looking more and more like Vivian's play, everything would probably work out. If Sarah were wrong, she would have to figure out something. And fast.

At the end of the aisle, the guy pushed her shoulder hard enough to make her stumble.

"On the ground," he shouted.

Her hearing had returned enough to make out what he'd said.

Another man held a similar shotgun near the pharmacy's drug pick-up counter. He guarded the four employees. Three were in white lab coats, and the other was the old woman from the front of the store.

"Is this all of them?" the guy watching the employees asked his partner.

"Yeah. No one else in the store."

"Okay, go and guard the front. I got them. Carlo is in the back. When he comes out, we'll load up and get out of here."

The guy who brought Sarah to the back didn't respond. He snorted hard and headed for the front of the store.

Now there was only one gunman in front of her, with Carlo in the back.

Five hostages in total.

"Hey, Carlo," the gunman yelled. "What's taking you so long? Hurry the fuck up."

He looked edgy, hopping from foot to foot. These boys weren't professionals. This wasn't planned. It was just three guys, jacked up on something, and wanting to steal drugs not available over the counter.

That gave this a more dangerous feel, unpredictable. Sarah wasn't close enough to a counter or an aisle to grab anything as a weapon. It had been a long time since she had felt this helpless. With these kinds of assailants, they were too crazy to provoke without something to back it up.

It would come to her. She would just have to wait.

"Carlo," he shouted louder. "You coming, man?"

"Leave the store now," a voice said from the back room. "And you won't be killed. Carlo is dead. Would you like to join him?"

The gunman's eyes doubled in size. He had to be on something. He probably wouldn't remember any of this tomorrow.

"What the fuck, man? You can't kill Carlo."

The gunman moved fast. He slipped in behind one of the girls in the white lab coats and used his free hand to pull up her hair. She cried out and protested but got to her knees. He held her in front of him.

Sarah's heart raced as she watched, helpless.

The man placed the tip of the weapon against the back of the girl's head and pushed her head forward. The male pharmacist went to get up, but when the perp jerked toward him, he eased back down.

"Everything okay back there?" the guy from the front yelled.

"All under control," the perp yelled back. Then he faced the pharmacy's back door. "Isn't that right, asshole in the storeroom? You killed Carlo. Now I kill a hostage. One for one. That work for you?"

The perp's eyes were wild and crazy. Sarah saw on his face that he was going to pull the trigger. She had to do something. The woman cried under his grip on the edge of hysterics. It was all happening too fast.

"Take me," Sarah said.

"Shut up," the perp shouted. "I got my dead girl right here."

She locked eyes with him. With no other ideas or options, Sarah stood up, conscious of how close the aisle was if he decided to shoot. It would be at least a five-foot dive for the cover of the aisle, but that held better odds than the woman getting shot for coming to work today.

"No. You. Don't," Sarah said. "I'm your walking dead girl."

"Yo, what the fuck you be talking 'bout?"

Sarah took a step toward him, ever conscious of the gun. At any second, he could just pull the trigger. Or spin to her and pull the trigger. An armed man is dangerous. An armed man buzzing on whatever drug was in this guy's blood was danger incarnate.

She took another step. He stared at her like he'd never seen a woman before. She kept her shoulders bowed and her hands out to show supplication and weakness.

"We got people trying the door," the other guy yelled from the front.

"Shoot them if they get inside," the guy watching Sarah yelled back.

She was passing the base of aisle three. One more aisle, and she would be in grabbing distance.

The perp didn't wait. He let go of the female employee's hair and kicked her away from him.

Then he aimed at Sarah.

"It's all good. I'll take you instead. I'd have to later if I don't now because you have big balls. Too big."

A blur of motion caught her peripheral vision, but she didn't turn to look. She locked eyes with the perp and waited for him to shoot, hoping whatever it was that came out of the back room was fast enough and swift enough to knock the perp down for the count.

"Bye bitch," he said.

It was like watching football on TV. One second the perp was standing there; the next, he was flying through the air in one of the most violent tackles Sarah had ever seen.

The gun fired, but the round harmlessly took a large chunk out of the ceiling tiles.

Sarah took a deep breath, not realizing until that moment that she had been holding it.

The man who jumped the perp climbed off, holding a metal bar.

Russell Anderson.

"What the hell?" Sarah whispered.

Just like at the warehouse earlier, this was the second time he had shown up to save her.

She wondered if this was a reflection of her ability. Was she weakening, and Vivian knew it? Who was this guy, and how did he know where to be and when?

"More people trying the door," the guy up front yelled back. "You want me to shoot them through the glass?"

The perp was out cold, blood trickling from a head wound. Russell bent over and retrieved the shotgun. He handed it to Sarah and dipped his head sideways.

She got the meaning and took the weapon.

Then she leaned in close and whispered, "Stick around this time. I want to talk to you."

She met his eyes. He nodded.

"Tell them to call the police," she motioned toward the employees and then moved away.

The aisle was long and exposed her to the front, but wherever the last perp was hiding, he wasn't watching the aisles. At the end of the row, she stood beside personal products for ladies. Without knowing where the last guy was, she would have to wait for him to come out into the open.

Ten seconds later, sirens wailed in the distance.

She waited, hunkered down beside the female pads.

"Hey, guys, you hear that?" he yelled.

At least two aisles over. He was in the painkillers aisle that led down behind the main counter. Still, there wasn't much she could do until he stepped out.

She waited.

"Guys?" he yelled. "What you want me to do? Aren't you all done back there? We gotta go, man."

Her breathing had calmed. She held a weapon. She was in charge again. This would defuse in seconds.

"Hey guys," the perp shouted, his voice hoarse. "What are we going to do here?"

"Too late to be asking that question, isn't it?" Sarah shouted back. "Toss the weapon into the open and then walk out with your hands behind your head, fingers laced."

"Who's that?"

"The only thing you should be focusing on is whether you toss out the gun or get shot. There's nothing else to decide here."

"Shut the fuck up. Who are you?"

"The grim reaper."

"Oh man, oh man, oh man …"

He mumbled to himself, his voice dropping to below a whisper. She lifted the shotgun, aimed it in the direction of the perp's voice, and waited.

The female pads beside her gave her an idea. The perp continued to whisper something. She couldn't have him run down his aisle to the back, where everyone sat unarmed. The police sounded like they were still a full minute away.

With a small green package in her hand, she lobbed it overhand to the front of the counter, where it bounced within ten feet from where she thought the perp was hiding.

She guessed right.

He jumped up into view and blasted a shot at the box of pads. Once he realized his mistake and swung toward her, she fired, keeping it low.

His jeans billowed around the ankles like a gust of wind hit him. The force of the blast knocked his feet back, and he fell forward. With his hands locked on his weapon, he couldn't get them in front fast enough. The weapon hit first, then elbows, and finally, his face bounced off the floor hard.

He grunted and moaned as he came to rest, curled up in a ball.

She sprang from cover. If he went for his gun, she would have no choice but to put him down. Before she could reach him, Russell jumped out of the aisle and kicked the perp's weapon out from under him. It spun in circles along the floor and smacked into the base of the front door.

"Why'd you do that?" Sarah asked, lowering her

weapon.

He looked at her, confused.

"I could've shot you," she said. "Jumping out like that. I was seconds away from kicking the gun."

"But you didn't, and I didn't want him," he pointed at the man writhing on the floor, blood seeping from his lower legs, "to get shot again. I don't want him to die."

"I'm sure he's glad you care so much."

Russell turned and walked toward the back of the pharmacy.

"Hey, where're you going?" Sarah asked.

"The police are coming. We shouldn't be here when they arrive. You have questions for me. The situation has been resolved. Now we leave."

"Really? Questions? Let's start right now. Who the fuck are you?"

Halfway down the aisle, he shouted back, "We need to talk. Just not now and not here."

"You're damn right we need to talk."

She followed Russell down the aisle, intent on knocking him unconscious if he tried to run.

There would be no more following her and showing up at the right time when she could use a hand. It was time to find out his story, even if she had to beat it out of him.

Chapter 17

Russell took Sarah to a quiet steak house that served breakfast. She hadn't eaten since the trail mix under the bridge while waiting out the rain. She had avoided the donuts at the police station, too. The smell of the restaurant almost overwhelmed her. By the time they took their seats, her hands were shaking.

He wouldn't talk on the way over in the cab. They left the pharmacy through the back door, against the wishes of the pharmacist who had wanted them to stay behind and receive some kind of award for stepping in and saving all of them.

But they had left, slamming the back door behind them.

She examined the scar on Russell's face while they waited for their food. The waitress had brought coffee and orange juice, but Sarah's orange juice was already gone.

With her coffee cup in hand, she studied the line down Russell's face and wondered at the pain of the original wound. She had injuries, too, but none that noticeable.

"I think you should start," Sarah said.

Her coffee was already half done. She motioned for the waitress to bring her more. Then she looked back at Russell, who met her gaze.

"I don't like this," he said, his eyes watering.

Sarah set down her cup, sat back in her chair, and regarded him with a dead stare, arms crossed.

"You don't like this? Then why are you involved? Why did you willingly walk into my life, follow me, and then save us all from drugged-up crazies? Huh? Tell me, what's going on?"

"I had to get involved."

"You had to," she repeated. "What compels you? What drives you to offer help? Why did you *have* to?"

"For it is written …"

"Please don't get religious on me."

"Why not?" he asked, his hands wrapping the coffee cup on the table. "What's wrong with God?"

"Nothing is wrong with God. After all that I've gone through, I know he exists. There just seem to be too many dark corners where he doesn't exist. Aristotle said it best."

Russell jerked his head up. "What did he say?"

"A painting needs the shadows to make it just right. Without the shadows, it would lack depth, character. The shadows represent evil on earth. It works for me in a morbid way. But I think I'll stop there. It's your turn to talk."

The waitress brought two plates of eggs and bacon. She set them down and asked if they needed anything else. Sarah reminded her about the coffee. The waitress apologized and stepped away. Before they could begin talking again, the woman was back, filling both of their cups.

After she was out of earshot, Sarah said, "You were about to explain how you're involved in my life."

She cut the whites off the egg, placed the yolk intact on a big spoon, then put it in her mouth, where she burst it with her tongue and savored the flavor as it covered the inside of her mouth.

"I hear things," Russell said as he fidgeted with the bacon.

"You hear things? I'm not sure I understand."

"Like they're whispered to me."

"Who whispers to you?" Sarah asked, wondering if Russell was talking about schizophrenia.

"My daughter."

"How old is she?"

Russell shot her a glance, then lowered his head and covered his eyes. He seemed to be overcome with emotion.

What's this guy's deal?

After a moment, he composed himself.

"My daughter, Penny, is dead."

"What? She's …" Sarah left it hanging as she continued chewing.

Russell nodded and bit into a strip of bacon.

"How?" Sarah asked.

For the next five minutes, Russell explained how Penny was stolen from the hospital and how Russell had given chase. That was how his face came to be scarred and how Penny was taken from him. Just when he thought his world was over and death was an exciting alternative, Penny began talking to him.

"Can you hear her now?" Sarah asked.

Russell shook his head.

Sarah realized how similar their stories were.

"I know about Vivian," Russell said.

That answers that question.

"How?"

"Penny told me."

"How does Penny know about my sister?"

Russell ate his eggs in silence. Sarah waited for his response. After a few moments, she continued eating, too.

"You eat your eggs weird," Russell said.

"I don't eat the whites. They have nothing nutritious in them. I only eat the yolks, and when I do, I love the feeling of the whole thing bursting into my mouth. Nothing like it."

"You're an intense person," Russell said. "You live your life that way. You eat your food in a gratifying and intense way. I bet you listen to music that way, too."

Sarah nodded. "Why not? If you enjoy music, crank it up, soak it in, and shout with the passion of the music you're involved with. That's the way life should be lived. At least for me. Others can do what they want. If you get bored easily, you're probably a boring person. I don't get bored." She broke her toast in half and bit into it. "You're deflecting, avoiding something here. Why did you follow me? Why were you at the pharmacy? How are you involved in my life?"

He set his fork down and wiped his mouth with the napkin. Then he set that down, placed both hands on the table, and stared at her.

"I was told you would be in town last night and that the text you were asked to send would have dire consequences."

"Oh yeah? For who?"

"You and me."

"Really?"

He nodded.

She set her toast down. "So that's why you tried to stop me?"

He nodded.

"And showed up at the warehouse to save me, and at the pharmacy, because if I didn't send the text, I wouldn't have had to stop a torture, and I wouldn't have had that headache?"

He nodded again.

"But if I didn't send that text, a good man would've been swindled out of lots of money. A marriage would've broken down for no good reason. How does that fit into your plan?"

"It doesn't."

"You're not making sense. Change that."

"Change what?"

"Start making sense. Don't piss me off."

"All I care about is you and your safety."

She frowned. "What? Why? I don't need another daddy."

"Penny is my daughter. She's family. I hear things about family and act on them."

"Tell me about the other times you acted on what Penny has told you."

Sarah pushed her plate away as she listened to Russell explain the pictures, how he sends them to Detective Collins, and how it was all related to family members, even distant family.

"Then how come you're helping me out? You're still not making sense."

The waitress interrupted to take their plates. Sarah asked for one bill.

"Do you know your family well?" Russell asked.

"What kind of fucking question is that?"

"How old were you when you learned about Vivian?"

Sarah wondered if that deserved an answer, but he had been forthright in explaining about Penny. The least she could do was answer this question.

"I learned about Vivian when I was eighteen, years after she was killed."

"Right, so doesn't that lead you to think that there are other family members that your parents have kept from you?"

"No, absolutely not. We've been very close since I was eighteen. If it weren't for them, I wouldn't be the woman I am today."

Russell leaned forward and clasped his hands together on the table. He stared at her.

"Your mother's sister's name is Abigail. I'm Russell, her only son. That makes me your cousin." He stuck his hand out. "Pleased to finally meet you, Sarah Roberts."

Chapter 18

AMANDA ADJUSTED HER BLACK sunglasses as she sat outside the steak house in her car. She watched Sarah and Russell through the restaurant window. From where she sat, only the tops of their heads were visible.

She tapped her fingers on her thighs and waited for her call to be returned. Someone had to deal with the two people that had thwarted Maxwell for over twenty-four hours. Their flow of money had been affected. Several people were dead, two of whom owed Maxwell a lot of money. Sure, he planned it that way, but the death of the other guys who were sent to deal with Tyrone and Mark wasn't in their plans.

You owe Maxwell money, and don't pay it back, he *may* kill you. If you murder one of his employees, he *will* kill you.

Amanda had started out five years ago as Maxwell Ramsey's girlfriend. What he didn't know when they began seeing each other was that she was an ex-kickboxer and cage fighter. He didn't even ask why her nose was crooked when they met. All he did was hold her and caress her like no man had ever done before.

Six months into their relationship, with Maxwell showering her with gifts and all the money she could spend, one of his men tried to cop a feel in Maxwell's office.

Maxwell lost it and ordered two men to take the offender outside. She had quickly asked if she could handle it. Curious and unsure, he had agreed.

Everyone had gathered outside, surrounding the offender and Amanda in a circle like a high school fight.

It didn't last long. She hit the man fifteen times in the span of eight seconds, five of those hits with the base of her foot. His coma broke one month later, and he walked out of the hospital two months later.

He was never seen in Vegas again. No one ever touched Amanda inappropriately after that, and Maxwell learned she could defend herself quite well. He had been quite impressed with her talents.

It wasn't long before she did odd jobs for him. They worked together now, running things in Vegas as a team. A husband and wife team. Although everyone still thought they dealt with Maxwell Ramsey, they were actually dealing with the two of them. She liked it that way. No one expected too much trouble when a girl was sent to collect a debt.

Little did they know.

She couldn't wait to get her hands on Sarah Roberts. Maxwell's contact inside the police station confirmed that a man they later learned was Russell Anderson had warned Detective Collins about Sarah Roberts being in town. Then Russell was rumored to have been at Maxwell's west-end warehouse. A BMW motorcycle, registered to Sarah Roberts out of Santa Rosa, was found parked a block from Maxwell's warehouse.

It was Amanda's idea to leave it there with a man watching it. Sarah would return to get her bike eventually, and when she did, they would be waiting for her.

But Amanda couldn't wait. She drove to the police station that morning and waited for Sarah, or Russell, to come out.

She had followed Sarah and stayed outside the pharmacy during the robbery. She thought she recognized two of the thugs, but that wasn't her concern.

Once gunfire erupted, she snuck up to the front window and saw Sarah and Russell walking toward the back of the pharmacy unscathed.

Whatever power they possessed to walk into a room filled with men and guns and be able to walk out every time without a scratch was a power she needed to learn more about.

Her phone rang.

"Yeah?"

"You have them?"

"Yes, darling."

"Good. I'll send men. When they leave, grab them both and bring them to the warehouse."

"I have a better plan."

Maxwell cleared his throat. "Go ahead."

"It's before noon. The steak house is busy. I say you call in a few favors owed to you by the taxi drivers of this glorious city. I know a couple of them owe you more money than they can pay back over five years." She switched the phone to the other ear. "Make sure you have at least two drivers going up and down in front of the steak house. Pick

Sarah and Russell up when they come out, and wherever they're dropped off, we nab them. Sarah is most likely going to go for her bike, anyway. We have men watching the bike, so she will be easy to grab."

"I like it. I'll call it in. If they leave before the taxis arrive, can you—"

"I'll stay on them."

"See, that's why I love you."

"This stuff makes me horny," Amanda said. "Be ready tonight."

"I'm always ready, baby. But listen, I'll be busy for a few hours. Have you got this?"

"Do you have to ask?"

"I know, I know …"

"What're you doing? What's keeping you busy?"

"I'm meeting with Detective Collins and then going to see Alfred to tell him the bad news about Tyrone and Mark."

"How do you think that'll go?"

"I think with how gruesome Tyrone's death was, Alfred will be more than willing to work with me on the deal. Mark still needs to be taken care of, though. He's languishing in that hospital, and that won't help me with Alfred."

"Kinda shitty how these two interrupted everything, isn't it?"

"I think it can work in our favor."

"How do you see that?"

"Mark is in the hospital. That puts Dr. Scott Emmet in a unique position. He's into me for a lot of money. He could bet that Mark Stead won't last the night. Since it is clear that Mark only suffered a severe beating and the odds are he *will* make the night, everyone will bet high on Scott to lose. Once

Mark dies, Scott gets paid on his bets. Then we get paid. The other side of this is that Alfred can see that I can get to anyone, anywhere, and at any time. He will have to sign me on as a partner. He will be left with no choice."

"You do have it all figured out."

"Just make sure those two stay away from the hospital and us. At least for today."

"Oh, don't worry. The morgue will be as close to the hospital as they'll get."

She disconnected and set the phone down beside her.

Sarah's head moved in the restaurant window as she talked to Russell. Amanda watched and cracked her knuckles.

"Your time is coming, bitch. Your time is coming."

Chapter 19

Sarah sat stunned in disbelief.

Her cousin?

She shook her head. "That's impossible."

Russell imitated her and shook his head. "No, it's not."

Sarah smacked the top of the table, rattling the utensils on the plates. A few patrons turned to look at them.

"Look, if my mother had a sister, I would know about it."

"Call her."

"What?"

"Call her. Ask her. But don't be all nonchalant. Ask her seriously. Ask as if you already know she has a sister. See what she says. I think you'll be surprised."

"Okay, to put this to rest, I'll call her. And when she confirms you're a liar, I will get the truth out of you. If this is a lie, it's the kind of shit that *really* pisses me off."

"Fair enough. Just call her."

Sarah retrieved her cell and dialed her parents. On the second ring, her father picked up.

"Sarah, how are things in Vegas? So good to hear from you."

"Are you all settled in now? How's Parkman doing?"

"Yes, we're settled in. Parkman's got everything ready to go, but since his client list is small right now, he took off for Maine."

"Maine? Why there?"

"It's the toothpick capital of the world. You should have seen him the day before he left. Researching toothpicks, running around our house one night when he came for dinner, spouting off trivia he had learned. Did you know that the toothpick is the object that Americans most often choke on? On average, almost nine thousand people injure themselves in some way with a toothpick every year. Also, did you know …"

"Dad?"

He cleared his throat. "Yeah?"

"You're sounding like Parkman."

"Sorry, just had him around the house for a few days before he left. Anyway, you called me. What's up?"

She looked across the table and met Russell's eyes. Could she see any family resemblance? Could she tell something like that by staring at him?

"I need the truth about something," Sarah said.

"Of course, Sarah. Ask away."

"Did Mom have any brothers or sisters?"

Dead silence met her question. For a second, she wondered if the line got disconnected.

"Dad?"

"Yeah, I'm here. Why would you ask something like that?"

"Oh, no, Dad. No deflecting. Does she have any siblings or not?"

"Wait, here she comes. I'll put her on."

"Dad …"

The line was pulled away. Tinny voices resonated to her as they spoke a few feet from the phone. Then her mother's voice broke in.

"Sarah, I'm so glad you called."

"Me too, Mom. I asked dad first, but he didn't get a chance to answer."

"What's that?"

"I asked if you had any brothers or sisters."

"Well, I …"

"It's a simple question, Mom."

"Why, though? What's the reason for asking?"

"I learned about my sister when I was eighteen. I just thought there may be others." She took Russell's advice and assumed that her mother had a sister. "Then I found out about your sister, Abigail."

There was a deep intake of air on the other end of the line. Her mother was moving, walking somewhere. A door shut.

"You okay, Mom?"

"Just give me a sec."

The man sitting across from her was probably her cousin. A man with a similar psychic trait as hers, but instead of writing down messages, he heard them and wielded those messages through pictures. Photos that helped the police solve crimes after they had taken place. She wondered who the enigma was now. Him or her?

"I do have a sister," her mother said. "Her name is

Abigail. How did you learn of this?"

"I'm having breakfast with my cousin in Vegas right now."

Her mother gasped. "Sarah, listen to me very closely. I said I have a sister. I did not say she had kids. My sister Abigail did not have any kids. Whoever you're sitting with is not your cousin."

Sarah leaned back and rubbed the bridge of her nose. Why all the lies? Who was telling the truth? She gave her parents a free pass when they withheld Vivian's existence from her, but why not talk about Abigail? Could she trust her mother after this? *Would* she trust her mother after this?

"Why haven't you told me about your sister?" Sarah asked.

"It's a long story. When you come home, we can talk—"

"No, now. I've got time. I need to know."

Her mother was breathing too close to the phone. That's all Sarah heard for the half a minute she waited. She wasn't going to be the one to break the silence.

Then her mother started. "The short version is, my sister and I didn't always get along. Then, when Vivian was kidnapped, Abigail didn't come out to help with the volunteers who had gathered to search for Vivian. I felt let down by my family."

"I know the feeling."

"I guess I deserve that." She paused for a moment. "Once Vivian was found, and we had the funeral, which Abigail *did* show up for, she drove home, and we didn't talk for a long time. She called me over a year later to see how you were doing. I told her that we hadn't told you about Vivian to spare you having to learn about grief at such a young age. I asked her to not even say the name Vivian until we were ready to tell you. Your father and I had a tough enough time trying to stay together in those days. You understand, don't you?"

"Go on."

Sarah's mother continued without hesitation as if now was the right time to unburden years of repressed secrets. "Abigail said she disapproved of our decision and wanted nothing to do with us if we were going to remember Vivian by forgetting about her. What she didn't get was that we weren't forgetting anything. We were trying to protect you."

"When was the last time you talked to your sister?"

"When you were three or four."

"Then how do you know whether she had children or not?"

"Because she couldn't have children. She babysat kids and even brought them on outings with us. I always thought she would've been a good mother, but things were wrong down there. Endometriosis or something. Doctors told her at twenty-five years of age that she would be childless. So if someone claims to know my sister, that's fine. But if they claim to be Abigail's kid, they are absolutely lying to you."

"Call your sister for me."

"Why?" Her mother sounded offended.

"Ask her if she had any kids."

"But she didn't."

"Ask anyway. Make sure you find out the truth. Don't let her lie to you."

"Why would she lie to me?" her mother asked.

"Doesn't it run in the family?"

"Sarah ..."

"Come on. What do you expect me to say? Just do this

for me. Call her. Then call me back. I gotta go."

When Sarah ended the call, her thumb and fingers went numb for a quick second. She opened her text program.

As fast as Sarah could type, Vivian dictated her next move.

Sarah didn't like it one bit.

She looked across the table at Russell. Because he didn't know how Vivian contacted her, he politely waited until she was done typing, probably assuming she was simply sending a text to someone.

Sarah wanted out of the restaurant, away from him and all the family drama that came with him. She needed to sort everything out. She needed to hear back from her mother before she decided what to do next.

"Where can I find you?" Sarah asked.

"Don't you want to talk about this?"

"Not right now. My mother is calling her sister. I've got something else to attend to. Then come find me, and we'll talk. And I need sleep."

Russell edged out of the chair sideways and stood.

"I got this," Sarah said, gesturing at the bill.

"Thanks." Russell nodded. "I'll see you soon."

She watched him weave through the tables and chairs. Near the front, he stopped at the waitress' supply nook, grabbed a handful of ketchup packages, then headed for the front door.

Why does he need ketchup packages?

After he stepped outside, she turned in her seat and looked down at the message on her phone.

Step outside. Get in a taxi. Wait three minutes exactly, then beat the driver until he needs to be hospitalized. Drive him to the hospital in his own cab. Get yourself admitted, too.

How the hell was *she* supposed to get admitted? And why did she have to beat the driver? That's gotta suck for the guy who happens to pick her up.

Even though she questioned some of Vivian's messages, Sarah always followed the instructions as closely as possible. Whether it made sense or not, she would do it.

For now, she wouldn't think about Russell and whether he was her cousin or not. She would put the fact that he showed up at the right time at the pharmacy and the warehouse in the back of her mind. When her mother called back, she would deal with it then.

Sarah motioned for the waitress.

It was time to go beat a cab driver. Then get herself admitted to the hospital.

Maybe she would get the sleep she needed in a hospital bed.

Chapter 20

MAXWELL RAMSEY REMOVED HIS sunglasses at the front doors of the police station. He had lived his entire life in Vegas. Many members of the police force knew him. Some of them even went to school with him.

The men in this building who knew him when they were younger knew right from the start that Maxwell would end up on the opposite side of the law that they were destined to be on. But after years of drug running, small-time violence, and robberies, Maxwell had gone legit. He had bought shares in an up-and-coming casino in downtown Vegas just off Fremont Street. After a few years of dividends and a couple of other financial ventures, Maxwell had enough money to live well and become one of Vegas's top money lenders.

The only difficult part of the job had been the collecting end of things. That attracted the wrong kind of attention. But without a show of force, people felt they could walk all over Maxwell. He had grown to hate lending money, but it brought in too much revenue to stop.

At least until the little casino on Fremont began attracting bigger crowds. So Maxwell purchased more shares. Finally, four months ago, he approached Alfred Carter, the current owner of the Fremont casino, who was searching for a financial partner with a deal. Sign Maxwell on as a partner in the business, and Maxwell would handle all the security and entertainment booking. All Alfred had to do was count the money—half the money.

Alfred had refused to just sign him on. He asked Maxwell what was in it for him. So Alfred offered a counter-deal. For five hundred million, Maxwell could buy the casino, and Alfred would walk away. There were two problems with that. The first was Maxwell didn't have that kind of money. The second, he didn't appreciate Alfred's attitude. So, Maxwell had been attempting to convince Alfred to sign the papers or lose the casino outright.

A fire had started inside the casino on three different occasions. A waitress was found murdered outside the casino's restaurant. A fat banker committed suicide inside one of the casino's hotel rooms. Although Maxwell had nothing to do with the banker, he was happy the man chose Alfred's casino to off himself.

The final straw was Maxwell's threat that Tyrone Percy, one of Alfred's long-time friends, someone he had tried to save from the life of crime, would be dead within three days, as well as Mark Stead. That was two days ago. He figured Alfred was chewing his fingernails raw at that very moment, waiting for Maxwell to call. If he knew what was good for him, he would have his lawyers present and the paperwork all drawn up to sign over half the business to Maxwell. Otherwise, Alfred wouldn't like it very much when Maxwell increased the pressure.

By the weekend, if Maxwell weren't a casino co-owner, Alfred's wife and his parents would have terrible accidents. Finally, if that wasn't enough, Maxwell wasn't above torture. Actually, he loved it and looked forward to the prospect of using pliers on each and every fingernail and toenail Alfred had. By the end of their session, Alfred would never walk right again, if at all. Maybe he would leave one hand unscathed so Alfred could still sign the documents.

At the counter, Maxwell asked to see Detective Collins. He was told to wait and that Collins would be right down.

Maxwell walked to the far wall and studied the pictures of the cops who patrolled the streets of Vegas. It was like a trophy wall of police officers holding awards and graduating from the academy. Made him sick to see some of the men he used to run around with thinking they'd made something of themselves by wearing a badge.

"Maxwell Ramsey," Collins said behind him. "What brings you to the police station? You're not wearing handcuffs."

Maxwell turned around slowly. He adjusted his light-colored suit jacket and flicked a piece of fluff off his shirt. Then he met Collins's gaze.

"Your sense of humor was never really that good." He moved closer to Collins. "I wanted to discuss Tyrone Percy and Mark Stead. I've heard things."

Collins's eyes twitched slightly.

You wouldn't be good at poker, Maxwell thought.

"Is this a confession? Should we move into an interrogation room?"

"Why you breaking my balls? We go way back. I was

there when you got messed up with that kid thing. When your girl wouldn't abort—"

Collins turned and headed for the main doors. "Follow me," he said over his shoulder.

Maxwell adjusted his suit again, looked around, and smiled, wondering if anyone had overheard him. He could break balls as hard as anyone else. With the appropriate amount of gangster limping, Maxwell followed Collins out of the building.

Outside, under the oppressive sun, they stared at each other through sunglasses.

"What was that back there?" Collins asked. "Why bring something up that happened over two decades ago? What's your beef with me?"

"You aren't too friendly these days. I come in asking about two of my friends, and you want to arrest me, embarrass me. I'm legit nowadays."

Collins shook his head and blew air out of his mouth. "You're not legit any more than lava is cold."

"What's that supposed to mean? I am a businessman. I pay my taxes." He looked at Collins from his head to his feet, sizing him up. "Or is it the level of success you're upset about? What's a detective make, huh? I probably make five or six times your annual income in one month. That why you're all up my ass when I come to have a friendly chat?"

"Yeah, that's it." Collins smirked. "Why are you here?"

"Tyrone was a friend. Mark *is* a friend. I wanted to see how the investigation is going."

"It's not my case," Collins said and started to walk away. "Go ask the detectives handling it."

"I'm asking you." Maxwell grabbed Collins's arm.

Collins looked down at Maxwell's hand and waited until Maxwell let go.

"You're going to have to read about it in the papers like everybody else," Collins said without turning around.

"Look, you don't have to like me or what I do. In fact, you can hate me." Maxwell moved around Collins and faced him. "But I live here and work here, just like you. Those were my friends." He loved acting and hoped Collins couldn't see through this performance. "Tyrone used to work for Big John, which means he worked for me. Only a couple of months ago, Tyrone was at my place, enjoying drinks with the missus and me. But now he's dead. I heard that he was cut into little pieces. What's up with that? Who would do that sort of thing? Sickos, man."

"You've heard a lot in a short time."

"Word travels fast. You know that."

Sweat beaded on Collins's forehead. He wiped it away with a handkerchief.

"I can't tell you anything, even if I knew. It's an active investigation."

"Do you guys have any suspects?"

"Yeah, one."

"Who?"

"Can't say."

Maxwell regarded him for a moment. "You're fucked, you know that?"

"Is that a threat or an observation?"

"You're lying to me. You don't have any idea who killed my friend last night and who tortured Mark."

"Okay, then we don't. Wish I could've helped you."

Collins turned and walked back toward the building.

"You always this sarcastic with members of the public?" Maxwell shouted after him.

Collins stopped at the door and looked back at Maxwell.

"Only legitimate gangsters who think they're actually contributing members of society. Those are the ones who I save all my sarcasm for. But don't worry, Mr. Ramsey, we'll find who hurt your friends, and when we do, he will go to prison for a long time. Or maybe he'll choose another option."

"What option?"

"Death by cop."

Collins shut the door and disappeared inside.

"Motherfucker," Maxwell mumbled as he stepped off the sidewalk and started for his car. "Death by cop. You worded that wrong. It's the death of a cop, asshole."

Chapter 21

Sarah paid the waitress and was outside fast enough to see Russell get in a yellow cab a block away. The driver made a U-turn and drove by the front of the steak house. As it passed, Sarah caught a glimpse of the driver wearing a red baseball cap and thought how lucky he was that he didn't pick up Sarah.

A part of her rebelled at the thought of randomly beating up a taxi driver. But Vivian would know what was happening and why. There were times the messages just didn't make sense, times when performing a task for Vivian seemed morally wrong. Yet all the messages had been to stop criminals and protect the innocent, so she would do as the messages asked, each and every time, without question.

She was innocent once. She wasn't protected when her neighbor violated her. Nor was Vivian.

Memories of those moments when she was eight years old fluttered behind her eyes like a bird locked in a room, smacking against the window to get out.

It was the reason she hated cops, even though she knew her hatred wasn't rational. That they would allow one of their own to violate her in such a way at such an early age had nothing to do with protect and serve. No wonder by the time she was nine, she was depressed, lost color in her complexion until she looked like a cadaver and started pulling out her hair.

She had been a victim of trichotillomania until she stopped pulling when she found her true purpose in life again when her will to live was resurrected at eighteen after being kidnapped. It was then that her life was saved—under conditions that could have killed her.

Now in her twenties, she was healthy, vibrant, and ready to fight for her sister.

She blinked in the sun and stepped off the sidewalk by the restaurant's front windows in search of a cab.

"Who gets to be the lucky taxi driver?" she murmured to herself as she walked past parked vehicles, heading toward the road.

Five vehicles ahead, a car door opened, and a woman got out. Sarah slowed, then stopped. The well-built woman leaned on the roof of her car with arms that had to pump iron. Sarah couldn't detect an ounce of fat on her anywhere. The skin-tight pants and the tight tank top showed everybody exactly what she owned underneath. Sarah could tell this woman wasn't shy about letting the world know the level of discipline involved in sculpting a body such as hers.

"Do I know you?" Sarah asked as she started walking again.

The woman shook her head. "I don't think so."

"With the way you're staring, maybe you've mistaken

me for someone else?"

The woman didn't respond as Sarah walked by her.

"No mistake," the woman said.

She stopped and looked back at her.

What the hell?

The woman checked her car door, then headed toward the restaurant without looking back.

The heat has to be getting to people.

In her business, Sarah could never be too careful. At any time, an old enemy of Armond Stuart's, Rod Howley's, or Hank Frommer's could pop up and take a shot at her. Watching her back and being paranoid came with what she did.

A yellow cab moved along the road slowly. The woman had entered the steak house and disappeared. The cab was getting closer.

Sarah jogged to the road and waved the cab over.

"I hope this is the one, Vivian," she said under her breath.

She slipped inside behind the driver and closed the door.

"Where to?" the driver asked.

His face caught her attention right away. The air conditioning was on full, yet the man was sweating buckets. His eyes in the rearview mirror looked panicked.

"West end of Vegas."

The cab started away.

"Do you have an address?" he asked.

She almost forgot to check the time. At least fifteen seconds had elapsed before she got her phone out.

"Just a second. I'll look it up."

The cab made a U-turn and started back toward where she and Russell had walked earlier. Maybe the driver knew an easier way to the west end.

"I can get the address in a couple of minutes. Just start heading toward the west end. I'll tell you where I'm going as we get closer."

The driver nodded.

They stopped at a light. The driver looked back a few times. Their eyes met. It was like he knew what was coming.

Less than two minutes left.

She looked out the window, not wanting to see his face. A chill went through her. The air in the back of the cab had to be below freezing. But it didn't matter. In a minute, she would be getting out.

The part of the message that said *get yourself admitted too* deeply disturbed her. How the hell was she supposed to get hospitalized? And what for? She hated hospitals. Spent too much time in them over the past few years.

But now she was supposed to be hospitalized.

The cab drove under a bridge, and Sarah saw the hospital coming up on their left.

Could he know?

She looked at the mirror again, but he stared through the windshield.

Thirty seconds left.

"This isn't west," she said.

"I have a quick fare I have to pick up at the police station."

"What? I'm your fare."

The doors locked.

She tried the back door, but it didn't budge.

"What's this?"

He glanced through his mirror at her. "A man is waiting

to meet you. Don't worry."

Her cell phone said twelve seconds left.

"What's his name?" Sarah asked.

"Maxwell Ramsey. He asked me to bring you to him at the police station. We will be there in a sec."

Her cell phone clock hit three minutes.

The driver turned right, away from the hospital. They hadn't gone five feet before Sarah leaned forward in her seat, grabbed the hair on the side of the man's head, pulled him to the right, and then rammed his head into the driver's side window.

Something cracked. She briefly wondered if it was the window or the man's head.

Before she could smash his head again, he slumped in his seat. The car slowed and angled to the right. It hopped up on the curb and stopped in a thicket of bushes.

Two cars were slowing to see what had happened. Sarah hopped over the front seat and exited from the passenger side. After running around the back of the cab, she gently opened the driver's side door and caught the man before he fell out. Blood matted in his hair. The window had a red smear with bits of hair on it.

She shoved him across the front seat and sat behind the wheel.

"This is fucking crazy," she said out loud as she shut the driver's side door.

She backed the cab away from the bush, then angled onto the road. A man in a Malibu watched everything, probably wondering if she was hijacking the cabbie, but she didn't care. If he called the police or followed her, she wasn't going far.

She drove across both lanes, cut across the intersection, and entered the hospital's parking area. The cab's radio blared on and on, the dispatcher announcing different pickups and other drivers agreeing to grab them.

The female dispatcher asked repeatedly for Marcus. On the dash, Sarah saw the driver's taxi license and realized she was in Marcus's cab.

The dispatcher said that she was sending police out to his last known location a half hour ago.

A half-hour? He just picked me up four minutes ago.

Did Marcus not radio in her pickup? Did Maxwell Ramsey have something to do with that? That was why Marcus was so nervous. He'd been bought.

She turned down the knob on the radio and came back to the here and now. She had to get admitted to the hospital.

"But how do I do that?"

Should she ram the taxi into another car? But why? Innocents could get hurt. If needed inside the hospital for something, how could she do anything if her arms were broken? Or worse, her legs?

Could Vivian really want her to injure herself?

Signs for the ER directed her to the right. She followed them as the cab driver remained silent beside her. Hopefully, he wasn't too hurt. That would really suck if she ended up getting arrested for this after all that she had been through since arriving in Vegas.

Four yellow taxis were parked near the ER entrance.

Could there be that many people leaving the ER that need rides? Or that many drivers being admitted?

She passed the vehicles, drove a few car lengths away, in case they knew Marcus, and parked alongside the curb. After quickly checking the man's pulse to see that it was steady, she jumped out and ran through the double doors.

A woman at a little window was on the phone and writing something on a piece of paper. It allowed Sarah to examine the waiting room for potential threats. Nothing seemed out of the ordinary. A woman here, a sick man there. A small child coughing. On the side of the room by the window, three men chatted angrily with each other. They were probably the taxi drivers.

"Can I help you?"

Sarah spun around. "I was a fare in a cab, and the driver took a nasty turn." She acted distraught. "I didn't know what to do."

"Where is he?" she asked, attempting to look over Sarah's shoulder.

"He's still in his taxi. He banged his head. I think he's unconscious."

The woman picked up the phone. "Okay, ma'am, we'll have somebody attend to him."

She spoke into the phone for a second and then set it down.

"They'll bring a stretcher out of that door," she pointed. "Show them where he is, okay."

The door burst open, and two paramedics wheeled out a stretcher. Sarah jumped in front and walked them to the taxi. They opened the door and began attending to the driver.

The three men who had been talking animatedly a moment ago followed them outside.

"What happened?" one of them asked.

Sarah turned around. All three wore similar pants, collar shirts and were unshaven. Was it a requirement to not shave to drive a taxi in Vegas?

"He turned a corner too fast. Hit his head. Passed out. I drove him here."

"Yeah, right." The man snorted.

"You don't believe me?" Sarah asked. "I do a good deed by driving an injured colleague of yours to the hospital, and you suspect that I'm up to something."

The third man moved closer as the paramedics lifted the cab driver onto their stretcher and wheeled him away.

"This is the third cab driver in half an hour that has been brought to the ER," the man said. "Our dispatcher is going crazy and sending police all over the city as other drivers call in late. You must understand that this doesn't look good for us. We are suspicious of everybody."

That was a new development. How does this play into what Vivian was having her do? Three drivers?

"I'm sure this one is not connected in any way," Sarah said. Then she remembered Russell and his cab and wondered if he was involved in any of this. "Was one of the three drivers admitted to wearing a red baseball cap?"

The men exchanged a glance. It was all she needed to know. That meant Russell was either with Maxwell Ramsey or inside the hospital. Either option wasn't good for him. That must be why Vivian wanted her inside the hospital.

Something serious was about to go down, and Vivian wanted her there.

But she didn't want to get into a needless fight or hurt herself enough to get admitted. Having to take a fall to get admitted wasn't going to be without pain.

Before any of the three men could speak again, she slipped past them and started for the ER doors.

"Hey, wait. We weren't done talking to you."

Feet scampered behind her. One of them would touch her and try to turn her around at any moment.

The doors were closer with each step.

Didn't Russell say something illegal was happening in the hospital, and he'd given the information to Collins, who hadn't worked the case yet?

"Hey," one of them called from right behind her.

The automatic doors slid open in front of her.

A hand dropped on her shoulder. She moved to defend herself, but Vivian took over her body.

Sarah's hand went numb, then her arm. Before she could say another word, her eyes closed, and Sarah dropped to the floor, unconscious.

Chapter 22

SARAH OPENED HER EYES and took in the room. A standard hospital cubicle surrounded by curtains suspended on small white tracks. The wall behind her head was a drab color. The putrid smell of medicine and a staleness reserved for hospitals alone wafted through the area.

She leaned up in bed and examined herself. A plastic bracelet with her name and a number printed on it had been clamped onto her wrist. She had no injuries other than a sore spot on her knee which must have hit the ground first when she blacked out. She was still dressed in her clothes, and her cell phone was a lump on her backside.

She swung her legs off the gurney and hopped down.

What now, Vivian?

There was no message on her phone. She had done what her sister had asked of her but wondered what the next step was.

Nothing infuriated her more than being directionless. Once a task was assigned, she performed it. She was in control, then it was over, and she moved on. This *getting admitted* part lacked direction.

She peeked through the curtain. This area of the hospital didn't look too busy. A lone woman sat at a nurse's station. A doctor talked to a patient behind another curtain, his back exposed as he edged out.

Find Russell and leave. Maybe that's why she was supposed to get inside.

She moved out of her temporary room, walked to the next one, and pulled the curtain back. An old man with tubes in his nose lie sleeping.

At the next cubicle, an old woman looked at Sarah and coughed. Sarah apologized for getting the wrong person and dropped the curtain back in place.

This had to be where they admitted patients first. Either they stayed in the hospital and were moved to more permanent rooms or discharged.

That meant Russell might be in one of them.

She checked the next two cubicles, but they were empty.

The last one to check was the one where the doctor was still talking to the patient, but she was too far away to hear.

Another doctor entered and walked toward her. The doctor walked by without looking up.

"Can I help you?"

Sarah jumped. The woman at the nurse's station had noticed her. Sarah moved closer and leaned on the counter.

"My friend and I were recently admitted, and I need to talk to him. Can you tell me where he would be?"

"Did you try admitting downstairs?"

Sarah pointed at the cubicle area where she had been. "I just came out of there. We got separated. I need to see if he's okay."

The nurse looked upset that she was being asked to help. Sarah wanted to smack the smug look off her face. Her nametag read Clarice.

"His name?" Clarice asked in a nasal voice.

"Russell Anderson."

She typed on the keyboard, stopped, then typed again.

"I don't have a Russell Anderson in the system. Is that with two esses and two els?"

Sarah nodded, hoping that was the proper spelling.

"I'm sorry." Clarice raised her eyebrows. "There's no Russell Anderson in our system. You said you were admitted together?"

"Maybe he's waiting for me outside."

Sarah walked away, looking for an exit sign.

"But, ma'am, if he was admitted with you—"

She turned a corner, leaving the nurse's station behind.

What the hell am I doing here? she asked, frustration building inside.

At the end of the hall, she turned to the right, away from the exit. Until she got kicked out, she would wander the halls looking for Russell or anyone else she was sent there to find.

Doctors passed her. A nurse ran by her, a clipboard in her hand. Up ahead, an old man with an IV pole on wheels walked slowly toward her. As far as the hospital staff was concerned, she was just another patient—in street clothes— out for a stroll to break up the monotony of being cooped up in her room all day. Maybe she needed a gown.

She was grateful Vivian had taken over to get her inside the hospital. Painful alternatives were all she had come up with.

A door opened to a room halfway up the corridor. The hall turned at that corner so that Sarah could see inside. Even from twenty feet away, she recognized the man she had met at the warehouse after he had been tortured.

Mark Stead.

The door shut slowly behind the nurse who exited.

That must be the reason she was brought here. To talk to Mark. Find out who was after him. Who tried to kill him? Although, there was another option. He may see her and still feel it's all her fault. Then she would make him talk, feeding into his belief that she was in on his torture.

Once she knew who was behind everything, she could let Detective Collins know and leave Las Vegas. As far as she was concerned, her job was done here.

She was only ten feet away when the door opened again, and a doctor in a white lab coat stepped out of the room and headed down the hall in the opposite direction.

From the glance inside she got, the room appeared empty of all hospital personnel.

Perfect.

The hallway was empty behind her except for the slow-moving old man with the IV pole.

She walked as if she was supposed to be there, opened the door, and strode inside. The authorities must feel that the threat to Mark was over because no one guarded the room. She thought someone should at least watch over him while he slept.

The room was like any other and smelled of antiseptic. She wrinkled her nose and wished she didn't have to breathe while inside the room.

Mark's chest rose and fell with his rhythmic breathing.

His eyelids didn't flutter with REM. She could wake him, ask him a few questions, and be gone before anyone came back.

But she wanted to be on the other side of the bed to face the door.

She walked around his bed, picking up the clipboard attached to the end to see what she could find out. His feet were wrapped in gauze. Many parts of his body were bandaged. She felt sorry for the guy and didn't want to wake him up, but she felt this was why Vivian wanted her inside the hospital. It would've been very hard to get this close to Mark any other way, even if she knew he was here.

She gently placed a hand on his shoulder, the other on the steel bars raised on the side of the bed.

"Mark?" she said, shaking his shoulder. "Mark, wake up."

He muttered in his sleep and moved a little.

"Mark, wake up." She shoved his shoulder harder. "We have to talk."

He opened his eyes and tried to focus. She wondered if they had him juiced up on some kind of drugs.

He blinked a few times, his eyes unfocused. Then he fell back under.

"Mark," she snapped. "Seriously, wake up."

His eyes snapped open this time, and he turned to her. He groaned under his breath. Then tried to speak.

"What … what are you—"

"Who came after you? I need a name."

He moved away from her until his head hung off the edge of the bed, his face contorted in fear.

"I'm not the enemy," she said.

The door opened with a bang. Mark twisted in the bed to

see who had entered.

The same doctor in the white lab coat who had left Mark's room moments ago was back.

"Oh, I didn't know you had a visitor," the doctor said.

Mark shook his head. "I don't. Please, get her away from me."

This was ridiculous. She had stopped his torture and was only trying to find out who was behind it to save him any future issues.

"We were just talking," Sarah said.

The doctor moved into the room, the door closing slowly behind him.

"How did you get in here?" he asked.

"Through that door," Sarah said, pointing behind him. She kept her face passive as if this was no big deal, but her gut told her something was wrong.

"No, what I mean is, how did you get to this part of the hospital? This isn't visiting hours. This area is patients only."

Sarah held up her wrist and showed the hospital band.

"Please," Mark begged.

He looked absolutely terrified. There was no way she could elicit this kind of response simply because she showed up to ask him a few questions. Something else was going on.

"You're going to have to leave," the doctor said.

The bed separated the doctor from her. By the time they called security, she might discover why Mark was so afraid.

She gazed down at him. "What has got you so spooked? Tell me, who are you afraid of?"

"You," he stammered.

"Me? Why?"

Mark quickly glanced at the doctor and then back to

Sarah.

"I was told you orchestrated everything at the warehouse and would come here to finish off the job. I know Maxwell. He likes to use women as enforcers." Mark spoke very fast. He licked his lips and swallowed. "He says to use a woman belittles the men who are being hurt."

"I can assure you that I don't work for Maxwell. I have never met the man."

"Bullshit," Mark spat out.

The doctor moved toward the door.

"Who told you I was coming to finish the job?" Sarah asked.

Mark exchanged a glance with the doctor again, then looked back at Sarah.

"Go ahead," the doctor said. "You can tell her."

Something clicked behind the doctor. Sarah frowned and looked to see what he was doing. His hands were behind his back, and he was leaning against the door. She wasn't sure, but she thought he had just locked the door.

Mark nodded toward the doctor. "He told me."

Everything Russell told her about the pictures he had sent to Detective Collins and how Collins hadn't done anything about the hospital betting ring regarding which patients would die first raced through her mind. It all came clear in seconds.

Mark was to be executed with Sarah in the room. The doctor subdues Sarah, and all is well.

In his right hand, a large needle came out from behind the doctor's coat. Then he presented his left hand, also holding a large needle.

"Ahh, what have we got here, Doc?" Sarah asked. She

stepped away from Mark's bed, scanning for anything she could use as a weapon. She had found another moment when having her gun would come in handy.

A small phone sat on the table beside the bed. A few items were tied to the wall with cords, but nothing else was close enough for her to grab.

"Inside each of these two beauties is a clear liquid called Myristicin."

"Oh yeah?" Sarah said, trying to stall him. "What's it gonna do to us?" She bumped into the wall and looked out the second-floor window. Jumping would be better than dying by injection, but she didn't think Mark could get out of bed, let alone jump out a window.

Near his lower abdomen, a wet spot formed and edged out in a circle as he lost control of his bladder.

"Myristicin comes from the seed of a nutmeg." He smiled a wicked smile. "It even smells like the spice."

"And why inject that into someone?"

"Don't you know that nutmeg is extremely poisonous when injected into a vein?"

Sarah shook her head in the negative. The doctor hadn't advanced too far yet. He seemed to be enjoying the terror he was putting Mark through. Either that, or he was waiting for backup.

"At first, you'll experience chest pain, double vision, and eye irritation. Then the abdominal pain will start, followed by nausea—but you don't want to throw up." He wagged a finger at her, the needle held precariously in the other three.

Drop it, she willed.

"Don't induce vomiting. You'll go through convulsions, rapid heart rate, and seizures. That is, if you live long enough for all that to happen. Not many people get this much in their system at one time."

Mark was edging off the bed, about to fall to the floor on Sarah's side, when the doctor pounced on him and jammed the needle into the meat of his buttocks.

Mark screamed and slipped over the metal railing and off the bed. He swung around as he hit the floor and tried to rip the needle out of his backside.

Sarah lunged for the doctor.

She grabbed a handful of his hair. As she was about to yank his head back to punch him in the throat, he spun around and jabbed the second needle at her.

Sarah expected his thrust and pivoted away like she was rolling off a tackle. This time she lost her balance, tripped over her own foot, and hit the wall on her way to the floor.

Chapter 23

MAXWELL SAT IN HIS air-conditioned car and watched the street half a block down from the police station. No taxis had pulled up, and there was no sign of Sarah or Russell.

He pulled out his phone and called Amanda. She answered on the first ring.

"Where's the girl? Where's Russell?"

"It's under control."

"I'm sitting here waiting with my thumb up my ass. No one has shown up."

"What?" It sounded like she was pulling her car over. "How is that possible? Those guys owe you more money than they could pay back. No way would they deviate from the plan. They should've been there by now." Screeching tires emanated through the phone. "I'm turning around."

"I'm not even two miles away from the steak house. What could've happened?"

"I have no idea. I saw them both get picked up."

"And did they come this way?" Maxwell asked.

"Yes."

She sounded confused, which made it hard for him to be angry with her. But he needed results. Everyone knew that, especially Amanda.

"Find them."

"I'll contact their dispatcher. Maybe I'll learn where they went instead."

"Just find them." He jabbed at the end call button, breaking a nail.

***

Detective Collins grabbed Munro's arm before leaving the unmarked cruiser.

"You sure about this?" he asked.

"Yes, I am. We always talk about acting on our hunches."

"We haven't slept since yesterday. Instead of going home, on a hunch, you want to visit Mark Stead in his hospital bed to check on the veracity of his statement, although what you really want to do is verify a doctor named Scott Emmet works here and if he is on duty right now or not? Is that it? Do I have it all?"

"That's it." She shrugged off his hand and got out of the car. "That's my hunch."

He got out and slammed his door. "Then can I go home and sleep?"

"When we're done here, you can do whatever you want."

They started for the hospital doors and fell in side by side.

"Why now?" Collins asked. "Why not tonight or tomorrow? Why does this hunch have to be dealt with right now?"

"Because Russell made a point of mentioning the hospital tip he had supplied to you and how it hadn't been solved yet. If what he says is true, which you've discovered to be the case every time, then this hospital betting ring is a problem. People could be murdering for money here."

"Okay, but is there a reason we have to do it right now?"

"Yeah. Mark Stead was tortured last night and was probably supposed to be killed, just like Tyrone Percy. My guess, or rather my hunch, is that whoever's behind Mark's attack will want to finish the job as soon as possible."

"Well, that makes sense."

They entered the hospital, walked up to the first counter, flashed their badges, and asked for Mark Stead's room. They were directed to an elevator leading them to the second floor.

Following the blue line on the floor to the elevator, Collins asked, "And you think the man behind all this is recently retired loan shark Maxwell Ramsey?"

"One hundred percent."

Collins pushed the button to call the elevator. "Why are you so sure?"

"His visiting you at the station today was to deflect suspicion from him. He wanted to show his face and make us think he was truly concerned about Mark and Tyrone. But all the men involved in this case either worked for him or used to work for him in some capacity. He's the most probable connection. This just smells of Ramsey."

"And I thought this case smelled of shit."

The doors opened, and they entered the elevator. Munro stopped and peeked out. Then she shook her head, leaned back in, and hit the second-floor button.

"What was that for?" Collins asked.

"Thought I saw something, but it was nothing."

***

Amanda squealed into the hospital parking lot. After speaking with dispatch and learning that three of their drivers were admitted to the ER within the last twenty minutes, Amanda knew what had happened.

On her way to the hospital, she called Maxwell back. He said he would meet her there. He told her to get inside and find Sarah. But stay away from Scott, who had a job to do.

"But what if that's where Sarah and Russell are? Trying to stop Scott from removing our subject?"

"Let me handle it when I get there. Just watch your back. And how the fuck did they know they were being ambushed?"

"How did they know about the warehouse? How did they know to deal with Detective Collins? How did they know a lot of things—Maxwell, you there?"

But Maxwell had already hung up.

She angled into a parking spot, aiming the front of the car at the road with an unobstructed path for an easy escape if need be.

She exited the car and scanned the parking area. Fighting wasn't what worried Amanda. She loved to fight and had spent too much time doing it to worry about a few fists flying her way. It was weapons she hated. You can't fight a bullet or a knife once it was airborne and flying toward your head.

She locked her door, and half ran, half jogged across the parking lot.

Near the admin doors, an unmarked cruiser slowed and then stopped on the side. Two people hesitated for a moment and then got out.

Detective Collins and Munro.

Shit! What are they doing here?

She dialed Maxwell to warn him, but he didn't pick up.

As the detectives walked around their car and entered the hospital, Amanda picked up her pace until she was running to catch up.

She entered as they stood at the admin counter, talking to a nurse. All she overheard was a room number that started with a two. She tried to catch her breath behind a large fake plant while the two detectives followed the blue line to the elevators.

On the far right, Amanda spied the sign for the stairs. She walked casually to the door, then ran up the stairs three at a time.

She opened the door to the second floor slowly and stepped out. After a quick turn around a corner, the elevator the two detectives were on came into view.

She pulled her cell phone out and flipped it to vibrate.

It rang in her hand.

"What?" she whispered.

"What do you mean, what?" Maxwell said through gasps of breath. He had to be running. "You called me."

"I'm on the second floor of the hospital."

"Have you found them?"

"No, but Collins and his partner are here."

"Why's that? I just left Collins at the police station half an hour ago."

"No idea, but they must've asked for a patient by name

because the woman at the front counter told them the second floor."

Both cops slipped out of the elevator and started her way. She turned and nonchalantly walked away from them. But now she couldn't see if they had entered a room.

Maxwell was screaming something into the phone. She ended the call and used the phone's screen as a mirror to look over her shoulder.

When she brought the phone up as if she were looking for a better signal, the detectives were nowhere to be seen.

She turned around.

They were gone.

Chapter 24

When Sarah hit the floor, she rolled hard and fast away from the bed. The doctor landed beside her, the needle dangerously close. For a brief second, it brought back horrible memories of the Rapturites in Toronto trying to inject her with their poison.

If she had slowed or stopped her roll sooner, she could've whacked at the arm holding the needle. Instead, she rolled again and then stopped at the wall next to the locked room door.

The doctor was already getting to his feet, the needle held out before him.

Mark had grown quiet on the other side of the bed. She chanced a glimpse his way under the bed. His eyes were shut, and he wasn't moving.

"Before we're done dancing here," Sarah said, "that needle is going into your face."

The doctor flicked a strand of hair out of his eyes. "Highly unlikely, little girl."

The use of the term *little girl* infuriated her. She wondered if she could turn around, unlock the door, and run into the corridor before she got injected in the back.

"Why go after Mark?" she asked. "Why was he tortured?"

"I have no idea, but I'm about to be paid a handsome sum because Mr. Stead is dead."

"Why'd you tell him I was coming to hurt him?"

"No idea," he said as he advanced toward her. "I was given your name and the message for Mark."

"By who?"

He edged forward again, closing the distance between them. He was close enough to dive at her. The door and the wall trapped her.

"The man I owe a lot of money to." He shrugged. "Actually, the man I used to owe a lot of money to. With Mark dead, that debt is paid. With you dead, I will *get* paid."

"You're talking about Maxwell Ramsey?"

A flicker of recognition crossed his face.

He took a large step forward and lunged, the needle aimed at her stomach.

Keeping her head and shoulders on the floor, she pushed off with her butt and lifted her foot to kick at the hand that held the needle. He was too fast. Her foot connected with his elbow, missing her chance to knock the needle from his grasp.

Before she could punch, roll, or move away, he was on her. He had to weigh at least two-hundred pounds, paralyzing her under his weight.

A scream escaped her lips as she writhed under him. He straddled her hips and wrapped his legs around hers, locking her lower body down. Her head bumped the door several times in her struggle to get out from under him.

He dropped his chest down on hers to avoid her flailing arms.

The tip of the needle came close to her face.

With one last effort, she pushed on his shoulders with both hands, but he didn't move more than an inch.

"Noooo!" she screamed in frustration. A rage she hadn't felt in a long time erupted inside her, and she fought with all her reserve energy.

The doctor jabbed at her. The needle plunged into the skin of her right arm.

The doctor's face contorted to a mask of insanity, his eyes wide, nostrils flared as he fought to keep his prey secure.

His big hand came to rest on the plunger.

***

Russell Anderson stared at the cop in front of him and wondered how he was going to get out of this. How could Russell know that a random car accident, unrelated to him and his task, would happen two blocks from where he was supposed to set up his accident? Things happen, sure, but he didn't anticipate that one.

When he distracted his cab driver with the red baseball cap, they were supposed to hit the light pole and get admitted to the hospital for observation after he complained of neck pain.

But it didn't work out that way.

As they turned the corner, just as he was supposed to

distract the driver, flashing lights caught the driver's eye up ahead. A yellow taxi was upside down in the middle of the road. The driver shouted something and hit the gas.

It was too late. Russell had missed his window of opportunity. But he had to be admitted to the hospital. He knew Sarah's life hung in the balance. She could die if he weren't there.

His daughter had told him so.

He had lunged over the front seat, grabbed the steering wheel, and yanked it hard to the right. The cab had sped across two lanes, hit the curb, and lifted into the air sideways. It rolled twice and came to rest on its roof.

Medical personnel attended to the scene, but they took too long. The driver was still unconscious when he was lifted out of the vehicle. The only problem Russell had was a sore right arm. He thought it was just bruised, but the doctor examining him at the hospital thought he should have an X-ray.

But Russell couldn't wait any longer. Sarah could already be in trouble or dead while he sat there talking to the police.

"Tell me again," the cop said. "Exactly what happened?"

Russell felt crowded in the little hospital room they had made him wait in, and the cop wasn't giving him any room.

"I already told you. My driver saw the accident up ahead, thought he knew the other driver, and hit the gas to race to the scene of the accident. The next thing I knew, the wheel spun out of control, and we hit the curb and flipped. That's all I remember. Now, can I go to the cafeteria? I need to leave the room for a few minutes."

Russell hopped off the bed.

"Hold up. I can't let you leave my sight until I'm certain

you've told me the truth."

"What else do you want me to say?"

"Sit back down. There's no rush. You're waiting for an X-ray anyway. Start from the beginning—"

"I can't," Russell cut him off. He was losing his patience. "I need to leave for a few minutes. I'm probably already too late." He turned toward the curtain.

The cop dropped a hand on his shoulder.

"Hold it right there. Why are you in such a hurry?" He turned Russell around. "I'm not *asking* anymore. Sit back down. The only reason I haven't handcuffed you yet is because that arm may be broken, but I will if you don't sit back down and tell me again what happened."

If Sarah died because he wasn't there for her when she needed him, even after Penny had told him what he was supposed to do, he could never forgive himself.

Family first.

That's why Penny talks to him. To protect family and make things right. He couldn't protect her when she was stolen from the hospital. Now, this was his chance to make things right.

Family first.

He turned until he faced the officer.

"I'm sorry," he said as he lifted his foot quickly. It connected with the cop's groin, lifting the cop off the floor.

The cop crossed his eyes. His mouth formed into a silent circle, and he doubled over at the waist, his hand coming off Russell's shoulder.

"I'm sorry," Russell said as he thrust the curtain out of the way and disappeared, heading to a room on the second floor.

He knew he was already too late.

***

Collins and Munro stopped in front of room 214. Munro raised her hand to knock but then stopped.

"What is it?" Collins asked.

"That girl. I recognize her."

Collins edged out and looked down the hall past Munro. At the end of the hallway, where it turned to the right, a tall, athletic woman stood reading something on the wall.

"You recognize her? What, you two go to the same gym?"

"Nothing like that."

"Then what?"

"When we got here, she was on the first floor. I thought she watched us go to the elevator."

The woman turned to look at them. Then Collins recognized her and realized Munro's hunch was correct.

"Holy shit. That's Maxwell's girlfriend, Amanda, something or other."

Amanda turned and started down the hall the other way.

Collins tried the door to Mark's room. It was locked. Something thumped behind the door, and then someone grunted.

Collins pulled out his sidearm and turned to Munro.

"Go after Amanda but be careful. Maxwell could be with her."

Munro started away. "What're you gonna do?"

"Get inside this room."

"Noooo," a female yelled from the other side of the door.

Collins knocked on the wooden door.

"Police. Open up, or I will shoot out the lock."

***

When the doctor lifted up to push the plunger, Sarah twisted her arm toward the floor. The doctor lost his grip. She dragged her arm under her, pulling the needle out far enough that when she dropped onto her back, she could grab the end and yank it out.

The doctor reached for it, but she threw it aside before he could get to it. The needle landed harmlessly near the bed, the clear liquid still inside.

Someone knocked on the door.

"Police. Open up, or I will shoot out the lock."

Sarah grabbed the top of the doctor's lab coat and brought his face over hers.

"Move away from the door," the man on the other side shouted. "I'm going to shoot out the lock."

"Shoot now!" Sarah yelled.

Then she shoved the doctor straight up as far as her arms would extend. He grabbed at her hands and tried to scramble out of the way, but she held him in a vise grip and screamed from the bottom of her gut. She turned her face away and squeezed her eyes shut.

Three loud bangs, like a hammer smacking solid wood, broke through her screaming and his shouting.

He jerked and vibrated in her hands. When she looked back, there were two red holes in the doctor. One was on his forehead over his right eye, the other on his cheek.

The door banged inward, slamming into her shoulder.

She let go of the doctor as his dead weight was too much.

He fell on top of her as the door smacked into her shoulder again.

"Hey, take it easy," she said.

"Sarah?" It was Detective Collins.

He eased the door open enough to squeeze through.

"What the hell happened here?"

"Get him off me."

Collins grabbed the doctor and rolled him off. Sarah took a deep breath and tried to calm her nerves. She shook all over.

"What the fuck?" Collins whispered.

"I know."

He glared at her. "What happened?"

"You need to know that this is your fault."

"My fault? How do you figure?"

"If you'd listened to Russell, come here, and investigated some betting scam the doctors were in, this asshole wouldn't have had a debt to pay back."

"What're you talking about?"

Footsteps slapped down the hallway outside the door. Russell appeared, holding his arm to his stomach.

"Sarah, are you okay?"

"Oh, were you supposed to be here sooner?" she asked. "Running a little late?"

She laid her head back on the floor and focused on catching her breath. That was a close one. Too close. It pissed her off that someone almost killed her. She would have to start carrying pepper spray around or start pumping iron. She could've knocked the doctor out before he got that needle in her arm if she were stronger. Or maybe she needed to return to Toronto and learn more martial arts from Aaron Stevens. She was sure he could teach her a thing or two—and she missed the hell out of him.

"Your arm's bleeding," Collins said.

"Ahh, a detective at work."

"Sarcasm's not fair."

"What's not fair?" Sarah asked. "You have a picture and a letter from Russell, and you don't investigate. Because of that, Mark Stead is probably dead now, and I almost bought a lovely farm."

"Okay, Sarah, I understand you're upset—"

"What's going on here?" a female voice broke in.

"Munro, come on in," Collins said. "Join us here at the scene of two murders."

Munro stepped over the doctor and walked around the bed to look at Mark's body.

"Collins?" she asked.

"Yeah?"

"You shot your weapon through the hospital room door and hit the doctor?"

"Yeah."

"Surrender your weapon. I'll call the firearms discharge investigation team in. Looks like you're in for some time off."

"What's going on?" Sarah asked. She leaned her head up against the wall.

Two nurses stood at the door, and a doctor peeked over their shoulder. Russell stepped back to give them some room.

"Once an officer uses deadly force," Collins said, "they can't work until the special investigations unit investigates. I'm in for a ton of paperwork and a little holiday without my firearm."

"I reckon that's going to be dangerous for you in this city," Sarah said.

Collins turned to Munro. "What happened to Amanda?"

"Couldn't find her. I ran back downstairs and outside. Nothing."

"Maxwell?"

Munro shook her head.

"Damn."

"Who's Amanda?" Sarah asked.

Collins rubbed his nose. "Someone you never want to meet in a back alley."

"If she has something to do with this, then it doesn't matter where, but I do want to meet her."

A doctor entered the room. "What happened here? Is anyone in need of medical care?"

Collins pointed at Sarah. "Her arm's bleeding. Looks like that needle jabbed her."

Sarah looked at the door where Russell had been standing.

He was gone.

Chapter 25

IT HAD BEEN THREE days since the attack in the hospital room. At that time, Sarah had finally gotten her hot bath and wine.

The first day was spent under guard at the hospital while her blood was taken. She remained under observation for a grueling twenty-four hours. Officers and detectives came and went while she rested. Statements were prepared and signed.

Russell didn't visit.

On the second day, her mother called back.

"Did you find anything out?" Sarah asked. "What'd your sister say?" It sounded weird saying those words to her mother.

"At first, she didn't want to discuss what she called 'ancient history.' In our first call, she told me she never had kids. Just as I suspected."

"Are you saying this guy is lying?" Sarah asked. "He's not my cousin?"

"No, I'm not saying that. Just give me a second."

"Okay, Mom. Spell it out for me."

"I didn't want to call you back right away. I had a feeling that Abigail was lying. Anyway, I was about to call her back when she called me. Sarah, have you ever had that happen when you're thinking of someone, and then they call you?"

"Seriously, Mom?"

"Right, sorry. Abigail called back to confess that she had a son out of wedlock."

"Okay, now we're getting somewhere."

"It really disturbed her because she had found religion and, well, anyway, she loves her son, but they don't talk much."

"So Russell's my cousin?" she asked. "Is that what you're saying? I have a family member?"

"Well, I don't know about that."

"What do you mean?" Sarah asked.

"My sister's name is Abigail Mercer. What did you say this guy's name was?"

"Russell Anderson."

There was a pause on the other end of the line. "Abigail's son's name was Michael Mercer, not Russell."

"Maybe he changed his name. Did she know whether Russell, I mean Michael, had any kids of his own?"

"Absolutely not. I asked about other family members. Was she aware of anyone else I could tell you about? We ended up having a heartwarming conversation. She was really happy you knew about Vivian—"

"Mom, I need to know if Michael had any kids."

"No. At least none that Abigail knows of. Her son lives in New York, last she heard."

Sarah had ended the call with her mother, who agreed to contact Abigail one more time to double-check if her son had given her any grandchildren.

At that point, the new information meant Russell Anderson was a liar. But why lie? Collins knew him. They were tied together because of the prophecies Russell offered Collins. What benefit would Russell have to lie to Sarah after helping her? Why bring her into their world? Most importantly, why was he crying when he asked her to not send the texts the night she arrived in Vegas?

Yesterday, after being discharged from the hospital, Collins and Munro had picked her up and moved her into a motel close to the police station.

Then Collins outlined what they had found out.

On the streets of Vegas, loan sharks thrived. One in particular, Maxwell Ramsey, was owed fifty thousand or more by Tyrone Percy. Mark Stead was involved financially with that somehow, but Munro hadn't gotten enough details to figure out the connection yet.

At the hospital, Dr. Scott Emmet was involved in a betting ring where the hospital staff would wager up to a thousand on which patients would die before others. More money was dished out if they could predict the day and even the hour. Emmet handled it all. Two nurses confessed to the whole thing, offering the names of all those involved. They were suspended without notice pending the investigation.

Emmet was into Maxwell Ramsey for over a hundred thousand. On the day Sarah showed up at the hospital, along with Collins, Munro, and Russell, one of the nurses took a call from Maxwell asking for Emmet. As far as Munro could gather from the hospital staff who were talking, Emmet had taken bets that Mark Stead would not last the day. Since he would obviously live, everyone bet the maximum against

Emmet. Some even doubled and tripled the maximum.

Emmet was looking to get out from under Maxwell's thumb and, at the same time, help Maxwell by finishing the job Sarah and Russell had stopped at the warehouse.

Sarah had asked the detectives how the cab drivers were involved.

They had something completely different going on. A dozen drivers were in on the 'vacation scheme.' When they were called out to pick up fares bound for the airport, they would load the luggage and get the person settled in the car. Then the driver would prescreen the fare to find out if they were taking a vacation or if business took them away from home.

Once the driver knew that the subject lived alone and would be away for some time, their empty house became a target. Two of the drivers had a long history of break-ins and robberies. These two professionals would be supplied with the address, and the time the subject was expected home. The break-in would take place, and once the house was emptied of valuables, the twelve drivers involved would meet and divvy up the findings. Sometimes they hit it big; other times, there was only a meager amount of pickings.

The two drivers were hospitalized because Sarah and Russell were into Maxwell for over ten thousand dollars each. Apparently, they would be given a free pass on that money if they delivered Sarah and Russell. The drivers were given Sarah's and Russell's descriptions. If they didn't deliver these people to Maxwell, the interest on their debts would soar to fifty percent.

That explained why Sarah's driver was so nervous when she got in his cab.

Since then, neither Amanda nor Maxwell had been seen. A state-wide bulletin had been posted for their arrest in connection with the murder of Tyrone Percy and Mark Stead. Munro had gone to see Alfred Carter, a casino owner in downtown Vegas with ties to Maxwell. All he did was complain about the extortion Maxwell was attempting on him to sign half of his business over.

His superiors authorized Collins to make a deal with Kristi Raine, Tyrone Percy's girlfriend. If she testified against Ramsey, extortion charges involving Jake Collins would be dropped. Bruce Collins's brother, Jake, was free to fly back to Phoenix, and his ID and wallet were returned. His money would remain in evidence pending the trial. Once that was completed, he would receive it back as well.

In the end, Russell Anderson, Maxwell Ramsey, and Maxwell's girlfriend, Amanda, disappeared.

***

Sarah leaned back in the rugged police chair, a coffee in hand.

"There's one more thing I'd like to know," she said.

Collins looked up from a document he was writing on. "What's that?"

"How much do you know about Russell Anderson?"

Collins set his pen down and swiveled his chair to face her. "What're you looking to find out?"

"He lied to me."

"How?"

"He told me we were cousins."

Collins suppressed a laugh. "He told you that?"

"I called my mother," Sarah said, ignoring his laugh. "Apparently, I do have a cousin. This is news to me. But my cousin's name is Michael Mercer, and he supposedly lives in New York."

Collins tapped the pen to his lips. "What're you looking to find out? I'd bet Russell is not your cousin."

"When people show up and tell me they know me somehow, especially if they say we're related, my guard goes up. I could tell you stories about a man named Jack Tate, who was actually Armond Stuart. Or Rod Howley, who chased me in Europe and, in the end, died saving my life."

"You would be awesome to have around a campfire."

Sarah looked down at her fingers clasped together on her lap. "No, my stories are unbelievable, and I'd cry like a baby at the good people I've lost, like Dolan Ryan and Esmerelda Hall." She looked up and met his gaze, her eyes watering. "There's too much wrong in this world."

"You're telling me."

They looked away from each other for a moment. Sarah took those few seconds to compose herself.

"So, if Russell Anderson misrepresented himself to me, I want to know why. If he didn't, then my mother's sister will be next on my list to visit."

Collins set down the pen on his desk. Sarah sipped her cold coffee.

"Are you off then?" Collins asked.

"As soon as I get my bike. It looks like you have everything sewn up here."

"We'll need you if this thing goes to trial."

"I'll be around. You've got my cell."

"What do you mean by around?"

"In the United States. Somewhere. Who knows. Just call."

"Do you have anywhere particular in mind?"

"Why?" Sarah narrowed her eyes. "Do you need to keep tabs on me?"

Collins raised his hands in defense. "Not at all. It was simple curiosity."

Sarah watched his face for a moment longer and then nodded subtly. "I was thinking of heading to Maine to meet up with a friend. A *cop* friend."

"Parkman?"

She leaned forward. "How do you know that name?"

"I looked into you. Did a little research. He's quite the guy."

"Been through a lot with him. I'd be dead without him."

"What's he doing in Maine?"

"Don't ask."

"Okay," Collins said and got up from his chair.

"It's a toothpick thing." Sarah placed her half-full coffee cup on the desk and stood.

"Toothpicks? Like the kind you put in your mouth?"

"Is there any other kind?"

"I guess not."

"Parkman's got a fetish for them. Makes him cuter."

"I'll remember that when heading out on the town. Girls like guys with toothpicks."

They chuckled and started for the door to the stairs.

"You sure you don't mind giving me a lift to my bike?"

"Not a problem," Collins said. Then he hollered for Munro, who was in a cubicle an aisle over. "Munro, I'll be back in half an hour. Just giving Sarah a ride to the west side."

Munro got up and stood at the door of the cubicle. "See ya, Sarah, and hey, thanks."

Minutes later, they were walking out of the police station and heading toward Collins's vehicle.

A yellow cab parked three rows over caught Sarah's eye. When she glanced that way, something moved in the front seat. She stopped and took a better look, but the cab was empty as far as she could see.

"What's up?" Collins asked.

"Oh, nothing. Thought I saw something."

They got in the car and drove off.

Chapter 26

Sarah said goodbye to Collins at her motorcycle, which was parked exactly where she had left it. He promised to stay in touch and call her as soon as he learned anything on the whereabouts of Russell Anderson or if he learned something of value when digging up Russell's history. Collins said he planned to do a family tree from all the government files he could get his hands on and see if Russell was his real name or not and if his family intersected with hers in any way.

Collins drove off, leaving her standing alone by her bike. Upon inspection, everything was exactly where she had left it. Even the helmet still sat on the back of the seat.

The only thing she had lost since arriving a few nights ago was her gun.

The warehouse where Mark Stead had been tortured was down the alley and across the road. It was early afternoon, the sun high and bright. Maybe the warehouse was open again since that part of the investigation was over. She could walk in the side door, go to the aisle where she stashed the weapon, and at least check to see if it was still there. What would it hurt? Otherwise, she would have to go through the approval process to get another.

Sarah felt naked without her weapon.

She set her helmet down on the bike and walked to the end of the alley. The road was empty of pedestrian traffic. The fabric warehouse looked like it was still closed. Yellow tape stuck to a bush on the edge of the parking lot blew in the soft breeze. The area seemed too quiet. In the distance, the highway rumbled softly. She took a deep breath and listened to her surroundings.

They hadn't located Maxwell or Amanda. Could they still be inside Vegas's city limits? Would Maxwell take that kind of risk, knowing the police were looking for him? And where was Russell? Was their disappearance connected?

She hopped off the curb and started across the parking lot as she recalled the taxi at the police station. Could someone have been inside the cab, watching them leave, waiting to report her whereabouts to Maxwell?

Halfway across the dusty parking lot, she stopped and thought about it. Were they waiting for her inside, and she had no way to defend herself, or was she being paranoid? No gun, no knife, no pepper spray, and no backup. As far as the cops were concerned, she was on her bike, already on the highway heading north toward Maine.

She should turn around, get on the bike, and leave. Choose the safer bet this time. No more fighting to stay alive.

But what fun would there be in that?

Fuck it. I want my gun back.

A bird cooed. A minivan raced by on the street behind her. She looked back. An old woman was diving. Sarah watched until it was out of sight.

She had no reason to suspect anything was wrong, yet her stomach told her something else entirely. She hated being jumpy, but Vegas hadn't really gone as well as she had expected.

At the side door to the warehouse, she stopped to listen. Nothing but a subtle wind. One last look at the road, and then she tried the door.

Locked or just stuck?

She pulled harder, and it popped open.

After a moment, with no one running at her, she opened the door wide, stepped inside the cavernous warehouse, and shut the door softly behind her.

The place looked deserted. So why was the door unlocked? Maybe she should call Collins back. He could walk through the building and check that no one was there.

With her cell phone in her hand, she brought Collins's number up on her screen and hovered her thumb over it for a second.

How would she explain trying the door? He would want to know why she was in there. Just hanging out, and having a look around, wouldn't cut it.

She slipped her phone into her back pocket. Better to get her property from its hiding place and leave town. Her presence in Vegas was no longer needed. What was needed was a little Sarah time. Vivian had been quiet for the past few days. Maine looked good right about now.

The gun was an aisle over. Her foot scraped the floor as she took her first step toward it. Something else responded to her noise. Was it an echo? A bird in the rafters?

She dropped low and scanned the immediate area.

Nothing moved except the hair on the back of her neck.

Someone was in the building. She could feel it.

If something was wrong, how come Vivian hadn't let her in on it? Then she remembered. Vivian can offer predictions and give Sarah a glimpse of the future, knowing Sarah would survive whatever it is Vivian's message entailed. But Vivian never told Sarah about her own future, whether directly or indirectly. If Sarah was meant to walk inside the warehouse and whether she found trouble or not, it wasn't Vivian's place to step in. By some celestial law, she was only allowed to direct Sarah to help others. Sure, she was harmed at times, but she would never perish by performing Vivian's messages. At least she hadn't yet.

The noise came again. A grunting sound came from the back corner where Mark had been tortured a few nights ago.

What the hell's that?

It was probably nothing, but she needed to know if Maxwell or Russell were there.

Maybe she should retrieve her weapon first and then find out. But she was already closer to the back than to her gun, so she moved that way, watching everything, waiting for someone to jump out like in the movies. She had sworn to herself she would never be the stupid girl who knowingly walked into the dark basement or stumbled through the wet forest, slipping and falling while she screamed. But sometimes, walking into the dark basement was the only way to root out evil. If anyone was going to do it, Sarah wanted to be the one. She needed to be. She had Vivian to back her up.

At the corner of the last aisle, she slowed. No other noises emanated from anywhere in the warehouse. It was eerily quiet. In minutes, she would have her gun, and ten minutes later, the wind would be resisting her as she raced along the highway out of Las Vegas.

A smile crossed her lips.

"Paranoia much?" she whispered to herself as she stepped out from behind the aisle.

"What the …?"

Russell Anderson, if that was his real name, was caught between two large columns of fabric on the second shelf of the back wall rack, at least twelve feet up. From what she could tell, the rolls had moved into him, securing his legs by their weight alone. With a little maneuvering, he might be able to pull his legs out, but if they were broken, he couldn't.

"Russell?"

His eyes fluttered. Then he opened them and tried to focus on her.

She started toward him. "Russell, how'd you get caught like that? Are you okay?"

He shook his head and nodded toward the exit sign.

"What?" she asked as she slowed.

"Oh, Sarah. It wasn't supposed to happen like this."

"What?"

"I'm sorry, Sarah."

Something scuffled behind her. She spun around and raised her hands in defense, but she was too late.

Something big and hard crossed her vision. Flashes of light streaked through her eyes as whatever it was crashed into the side of her face.

Chapter 27

Consciousness flowed back as if she swam up from the depths of the darkest waters. Her hands were trapped, unable to move, and her legs cramped. She opened her eyes, fluttering her lids. The floor had the faint copper smell of blood. Her blood.

A gash on her face had leaked out onto the hard concrete floor of the warehouse.

She moved her head slowly in case something was broken and looked around. Russell was still stuck between the two rolls of fabric. Ten feet from her on the left, a man with ugly dreadlocks and a tattoo on his face sat in a wooden chair, chewing on his nails. He pulled his hand away from his mouth, inspected his fingers, and then spit on the floor.

"Sarah Roberts," he said. "So glad you could join us."

"Maxwell Ramsey," she mumbled.

He placed his elbows on his knees and leaned forward. "You are good. You've been in Vegas all of three or four days, and you've managed to royally fuck me up. Can't say anyone else has accomplished that much before. At least not in such a short span of time."

She tried to shrug, but the restraints forbid that much movement. "Nothing personal."

Her cheek ached. It felt like the wound had sealed, but she worried talking would open it again. She hated facial wounds. Scars she could cover with clothing was one thing, but facial scars changed how a woman looked.

"Nothing personal?" he echoed her words as he got up from the chair. "Nothing personal?" He nodded to himself and stared up at the ceiling. "So then, I guess I should just let you go?" He faced her. "Since it's nothing personal, I don't have a beef with you, now do I?"

While he worked himself up, Sarah tried to see how she was tied. Ropes bound her wrists and ankles, and those ropes were connected behind her. An amateur hogtie.

"Don't you worry about that," he said. "You're not going anywhere until someone unties you."

Russell grunted and tried to push on the roll holding his lower leg.

Maxwell turned toward Russell. "How long have you been up there? Twenty-four hours now?"

Russell stopped pushing and stared down at Sarah. No one expected the two of them to be subdued in the warehouse with Maxwell as their captor. Everything was supposed to be over. Sarah wasn't even supposed to be there. The police were going to find Maxwell and arrest him. How did things get so far out of hand so quickly?

Russell's eyes were bloodshot and moist. He'd been crying again. It didn't sit well with getting them out of the warehouse alive.

"Have you ever jabbed someone with a fork?" Maxwell asked.

Sarah looked back at him. "What?"

"Have you ever jabbed someone with a fork? I mean, actually, take the fork"—he reached inside the back pocket of his jeans and pulled out a regular-looking kitchen fork, holding the prongs away from him—"and jab someone in the head with it, over and over until they bleed out." He made stabbing motions in the air with the fork.

"Can't say I have," Sarah said. The warehouse wasn't extra hot, but sweat beaded up and then rolled down her face, tickling her as it went. She lowered the uninjured part of her face and rubbed it on the floor. "I'm surprised no one has ever used a shovel on that ugly mug of yours. Just saying, sometimes people like you should be slapped with a shovel."

"Sarah Roberts." Maxwell tilted his head to look at her. "This is Las Vegas."

"I know where I am."

"You came to the gambling mecca of the world, and you rolled the dice."

"Well, actually, I didn't."

"Oh yes, you did," he said, nodding. "You gambled with more than you have. And it looks like you can't cover the debt."

"I don't gamble because I can't bluff very well."

"What?"

"I don't bluff, so gambling doesn't work for me."

"So what're you saying? You think you're going to walk away from this?"

"Absolutely."

He set his hands on his hips, made a grunting sound, and

stared down at her. "Pray tell."

"When this is all over, Russell and I will walk away. On the other hand, you will either be dead or in jail. That depends on how angry you make me."

Maxwell tossed his head back and laughed. A startled bird in the rafters went airborne at the sound, flapping its wings somewhere out of sight.

After a minute, Maxwell lowered his head and got his laughter under control. She pegged him as a show-off. Someone who needed drama in his life. He would have made it big on Broadway.

"I have men hidden everywhere. I knew you were approaching as soon as you set your helmet back down on your bike and looked this way. Those men are going to radio me if there's even a hint that someone is coming. No one is coming to save you as long as my radio stays silent. You're tied up, Russell is secured, and I have a gun. So, tell me, how are you planning on walking out of here?" Maxwell asked.

"Telling you that would be akin to showing you my cards. We're gambling. I think I'll keep that information close to my chest."

"Then I call your bluff and raise you." Maxwell pulled a silver gun out from behind his pants.

Shit. Not good.

She struggled against her binds with renewed fervor but to no avail.

Maxwell walked closer to Russell and raised his gun.

"I will save the fork for you, Sarah."

"Wait!" Sarah yelled. "What is it you want?"

Her wrists and ankles were chaffing. She had no choice but to continue to try to get out of her restraints.

"I only want one thing."

"What's that?" Sarah asked as she twisted to see Maxwell standing under Russell.

"I want you two dead for what you have cost me. Then I will kill the girl who plans to testify against me, Kristi Raine, and I will begin the arduous rebuilding process. If they don't have witnesses, they don't have a case. With you two crackerjack psychics out of my life, things will return to how they were."

"What about—"

The gun fired, cutting her off. Russell jolted as the bullet hit him in the chest. A small squirt of red popped out, surrounding the new black hole in his hoodie. Russell's face lost all color as his mouth formed a circle, and his eyes widened.

Sarah struggled, rolled onto her back, and fought to break loose, but the ropes were just too tight.

Maxwell laughed, his dreadlocks bouncing.

Then he fired his weapon again and again, Russell's body jolting as each bullet formed red dots on his chest. Maxwell stopped and tossed the weapon away when the gun clicked on empty.

Russell's head dropped, his chin resting on his chest. He didn't move again.

One more guffaw from Maxwell, and then he clicked his heels twice, pivoted, and walked to the gun. After picking it up with a white cloth he produced from another pocket, he wiped it free of his prints, stepped closer to Sarah, and knelt beside her. He pulled her fingers back and placed the gun into the palm of her hand, forcing her fingers around the handle.

"There, that should do it. When they find Russell's body,

they will also find this lovely weapon with all the evidence they'll need to see you killed Russell Anderson."

"Too set up," Sarah said, working hard to control her voice.

"What'd you say?"

"It's too set up. Any first-grade cop will see what happened here. Are you that fucking stupid?"

"Cuss at me. Get me going. I understand your methods. But don't worry. I'm not going to kill you. At least not right away. Someone else is coming to do that for me. She just had to dispose of your nice motorcycle first."

"Who's that?"

"My lovely girlfriend. I'm sure you'll find her quite exciting."

"I'm sure I will." Sarah had given up hope of freeing herself. The ropes were just too tight.

A door slammed somewhere in the warehouse.

"Ahh, there she is now."

Maxwell walked to the side and looked down the row.

"Everything work out?" he asked someone out of Sarah's line of sight. There was a mumbled response.

He stepped aside and made way for a young woman to enter. She was pretty, with a rugged face and a strong, athletic body. Something about her was familiar.

Then it came to her. The steak house that morning. As she walked out to catch a cab, this woman had stared at her.

"You set the cab drivers on us," Sarah said.

The woman turned to Maxwell. "She's good." Then she looked back at Sarah. "Untie her."

Maxwell moved toward Sarah. "It's your show, hun."

"So what, she calls the shots?" Sarah asked.

"That lip of yours," the woman said. "I'm going to knock it right the fuck off."

Maxwell was already loosening the binds on her wrists.

"You can try. Others have, but no one has succeeded yet."

"Today is the day you will learn to play in your own backyard. Coming to Vegas was a huge mistake for you."

"Somehow, I don't think so."

Maxwell went to work on her ankles. Seconds later, she was completely untied. Maxwell moved away from her fast.

Smart.

"Come on, bitch," the woman said. "Show me what you got."

Sarah was done with the big talk. Showing off and bravado wouldn't win this fight. Raw anger and quick thinking would. The woman in front of her looked strong and able to handle herself. Maxwell wouldn't let her loose on Sarah if he wasn't fairly confident she could manage the situation.

Whether Russell was her cousin or not, he had a big heart, and he had saved her from danger a couple of times since she had been in Vegas. She owed him a lot and would never get to repay him now. She couldn't let Russell die for nothing. This was her chance to pay them back.

The woman moved in, bouncing on the balls of her feet. Sarah feinted left but then hopped to the right and swung hard at the woman's face. So hard that when her fist met with empty air, she swung around in a full circle. For a brief second, her back was to the woman. She expected a fist in the kidneys or a foot in the small of her back, but nothing came.

"That all you got?" the woman asked.

Sarah drove herself forward, head low. With almost no time to react, the woman folded into Sarah's shoulder as she connected. Sarah's feet came off the ground and lifted above her head. Then the sensation of falling. At the last second, she got her hands in front of her and broke the fall, her right shoulder taking the weight.

The woman had absorbed the blow in her abdomen as she brought her hands around to Sarah's midsection and bent at the waist. Then she lifted Sarah and dropped her on her head.

Pain flared in Sarah's head and neck. She saw stars for a moment and had to shake her head to clear them.

A shadow covered her vision.

Sarah jerked her head back and out of the way as the woman's boot slammed on the floor an inch from Sarah's nose.

That was close.

She wished Aaron Stevens would walk in right then. He would know how to deal with a fighter like this woman.

Sarah rolled twice and then jumped to her feet.

The second she did, she dove sideways as the woman was already in the air, her foot extended in some kind of kickboxing move.

Street fighting could be very effective, but scrapping with a professional fighter, trained in the moves and countermoves of a martial artist or kickboxer, street fighting was lazy and sloppy.

When the woman landed, she turned and jumped again. Sarah felt she had to constantly move and let this woman land wherever she may be headed.

But this time, Sarah didn't move. As the woman came

down, her foot pointed at Sarah's face. Sarah dodged left just enough for the boot to pass without hitting its target. She swung her elbow up in a semicircle toward the woman's face.

Even though it was a fast move and unexpected, the woman somehow saw it coming. Her open palm wrapped around Sarah's elbow and allowed its forward momentum. She spun into Sarah in some kind of judo move, clamped onto Sarah's arm just below the shoulder, and then lifted upward. Less than a second later, Sarah was airborne, flying over the woman's back as she flipped her.

She landed hard, the wind knocked out of her.

Maxwell clapped and shouted on the side.

Sarah was outmatched. If she survived this, martial arts lessons would be in her near future.

She struggled to catch a breath while keeping her eyes on the woman. Maxwell and his girlfriend embraced and kissed.

"Well done, Amanda," Maxwell said. "I love to watch you fight." He looked down at Sarah. "You didn't even get one hit in. Pathetic."

She was breathing easier. Should she roll away, get to her feet, and run? Staying and fighting with Amanda, the machine, would only get her killed. The gun was emptied into Russell. Did they have any other weapons?

"Now for the fun part," Maxwell said.

Sarah made to get up, but Amanda pounced. She straddled Sarah and locked her arms down. With a swiftness that her eyes couldn't register, Amanda drove her fists into Sarah's stomach at least five times. Then she landed one left and one right punch across Sarah's cheeks, opening the wound on Sarah's face.

Pain flared up from the injured cheek. Blood covered

Amanda's bare fists.

"Are you done?" Sarah asked through a mouth filling with blood. This was the first time in her life she was convinced she couldn't beat the person she was fighting.

"Not yet, little bitch," Amanda said.

Sarah's eyes watered. She tried to blink it away. Being this helpless was maddening. She had fought bigger, stronger men and walked away. How could this woman be so fast?

Maxwell walked around her head. He was up to something. This would be her last chance. It was now or never.

Sarah yanked hard and got her right arm loose. She grabbed the woman's throat. Before she could squeeze or push in on the trachea, Amanda's rock-hard fist came down on Sarah's nose. Blood shot out of her face. Her eyes watered, and the pain hit extreme levels. It felt like her nose was broken. She moaned loud and hard, willing the pain to stop.

There was almost no way to see her attacker now as her eyes filled against her will. She had to get past it and fight, or she wouldn't walk out of the warehouse.

Instead of holding her nose, she moved her hands to her eyes, wiped them, and stared up at Amanda, who had started to climb off.

"She's ready now," Amanda said. "There's not much fight left in this one."

"Perfect," Maxwell said.

Sarah wiped at her eyes once more.

Maxwell moved in and got down on one knee. Something jabbed her above the left knee. It felt like a large bee sting. She screamed out and lifted her head to look.

The handle of the silver fork stuck out of her leg, the prongs submerged in her skin.

She screamed again. "What the fuck!"

"I asked if you had ever jabbed anyone with a fork."

Sarah reached for it, but he slapped her hand away.

"I've always wanted to see if I could kill someone with just a fork. Next, I will jab you a couple of times in the stomach, the chest, and the head, and finally, I will embed the fork in your heart. Isn't that great news? All this pain will be over in a few minutes."

Sarah screamed and reached for the fork again. She grabbed the handle and tried to pull it out, but the pain stopped her as she reared her head back and let out a wail.

The fork was ripped from her flesh in a violent pull.

She rubbed her eyes, opened them, and saw Maxwell above her. His smile was demonic. He moved Sarah's shirt up, exposing her stomach and bra. Amanda came to stand behind her and grabbed her arms, wrenching them back. All Sarah had left to defend herself were her legs, but to move her injured one was torture.

Why hadn't Vivian warned her of this? Could she get to her gun? Was there a way out of this that she couldn't see yet?

Maxwell rubbed his hand along her naked stomach and then up onto her breast. He squeezed.

Sarah thought she would vomit on him. The bloody fork rose up in his hand.

"Now, to impale such a pretty stomach. Such a pity you have to die. I could use you on the streets for a while. But not now. You have to die, Sarah Roberts. You're too much trouble. Goodbye."

He grunted as he swung his arm down hard.

A gun fired somewhere in the warehouse.

Blood splattered across her face and covered her vision. The fork missed its mark, jamming harmlessly into the floor beside her. Then the wind was knocked from her again as a weight slammed onto her.

Her hands were released. Amanda screamed. Sarah squeezed her eyes shut as she pushed against the body on her, trying to move out from under it as she breathed through her nose. She couldn't believe how watery her eyes were.

A gun fired again.

Whoever was firing wasn't aiming at Sarah. Amanda yelled from farther away now. She opened her eyes enough to see Maxwell on her. He was heavy, but she managed to get out from under him. Walking would be difficult with the leg wound, but she had to find a way to get to her gun a few aisles over.

Whoever was out there couldn't possibly be a friend of hers. It couldn't be the police because Maxwell's guards didn't warn him. Maybe one of his guards was seeking revenge for something.

Whatever the reason, all that mattered now was her gun.

She rubbed her eyes with her shirt and tilted her head back to stanch the blood flow from her ruined nose.

Maxwell's shooter was chasing Amanda through the warehouse. Sarah dragged herself a few feet until she could reach the racks that held the rolls of fabric.

She pulled herself up to a sitting position. Then, with her good leg under her, she got onto her feet. Blood oozed from her leg wound, but thankfully, it wasn't much.

The gun fired again, followed by a short yelp. It sounded

like Amanda got hit.

That meant the shooter would be coming after Sarah next.

With the rack in her grip for balance, she hopped to the side. As fast as she could without falling, she hopped up to the aisle where her gun was stashed.

Someone was coming. Footsteps resounded through the quiet warehouse. It was either Amanda or the shooter. Whoever it was, she would need her gun.

She hopped along the aisle as fast as her good leg would take her.

The two rolls where she'd stashed the weapon appeared to be untouched.

The footsteps drew closer.

She reached inside and felt around for her gun.

It wasn't there.

She was sure this was the spot. Digging deeper produced nothing. Her hands came up empty.

"Looking for this?" a man said behind her.

She froze. Blood trickled from her nostrils as she waited for the bullet. When none came, she kept her hands visible and turned around.

Russell Anderson stood at the end of the aisle, holding her gun by the barrel.

"Here, take it," he said. He stumbled into the rack and dropped to his knees. His shoulders heaved as he sobbed. The gun slipped from his grasp and slid to a stop along the floor.

Sarah hobbled to his side.

"I thought you were dead. I saw Maxwell shoot you. What the hell's going on?"

"Vest." He coughed and scrunched up his face.

"Vest?" She was surprised at how nasal her voice sounded. "You're wearing a vest?"

"It hurts." He dropped his head and closed his eyes. "I've never been shot before. My daughter told me to take those ketchup packets from the steak house that morning when we had breakfast. Then I taped them to the Kevlar vest here." He wiped the tears off his cheeks and opened his hoodie at the front. "She said I would be shot and that if I didn't do this," he stopped and met Sarah's eyes, "that you would die today. I couldn't let that happen. I can't let my family die. Never again. That's why when I first saw you, I cried when I asked you to not send the text. I already knew that you would die if I didn't get shot. I was afraid that I wouldn't be able to come through for you. Then your death would be on my head."

Sarah stepped away and used the rack for support. "I guess I should say thanks for getting shot. Looks like you saved both of us. How did you get out?"

"They weren't securing me. It only looked that way. When Maxwell came in yesterday and saw me like that, he decided to leave me alone until he captured you and brought you here. Then you walked in on your own. Penny told me where you hid your gun."

"I'm not your family. We're not cousins. Abigail did have a son. You were right about that. But his name was—"

"Michael Mercer?" He nodded. "That was my name before I changed it to Russell Anderson. I left New York in search of my real father. The trail led me to Las Vegas but stopped there. I got my girlfriend pregnant and decided to stay and raise Penny."

"If what you're saying is true, then your mother does not know about your daughter."

He nodded again. "No one in my family, our family, knows about Penny. My mother would've never approved. Instead of being shunned, I walked away. She still thinks I live in New York."

Distant sirens shrieked on their way to the warehouse. Sarah's injuries made her want to lie down and wait.

"How can I ever believe you? How can I ever believe anyone in this family?"

"I have proof."

She turned toward him. "You have proof?"

He pulled a photo from his back pocket and extended it to her.

Sarah took it from him.

"Who are these people?" she asked, even though she thought she recognized herself at two years old.

"That's your mother, Amelia, and her sister, my mom, Abigail. The three children are you, me, and Vivian."

Sarah brought the photo closer. After being told who the people were, she easily recognized her mother and the family resemblance in Abigail. Russell was also recognizable.

But Vivian … this was the only shot of Vivian she had ever seen.

Vivian's face shone in the photo as she smiled wide, holding little Sarah's hand and carrying a bucket and shovel to play with in the sand on the beach wherever the photo was taken.

Sarah's eyes were already watery, mixing with the tears she shed for Vivian.

The sirens stopped outside, and the door banged open a second later. Heavy footsteps rushed inside the warehouse.

"Over here," Russell shouted, then moaned and held his

chest.

"Can I keep this?" Sarah asked.

Russell nodded. "I brought it for you."

Collins ran up their aisle.

"I leave you alone for …" He paused, then asked, "What happened here?"

"Maxwell and his girlfriend had a little chat with us."

"Detective Collins?" someone shouted a few aisles over. "We have two people down. Appears to be gunshot wounds."

"A talk, eh?"

Chapter 28

AFTER A BRIEF HOSPITAL stay where the doctors set Sarah's nose and stitched up her leg and face, she spent countless hours giving her statement. In Russell's statement, they wanted to know how he came to be wearing a bulletproof vest and ketchup packets. Only Detective Collins understood the psychic connection and did his best to help explain it away.

No charges were laid against either Sarah or Russell in the death of Maxwell Ramsey and his girlfriend, Amanda.

They found Sarah's bike on a trailer at the back of the warehouse. Maxwell's men had abandoned the area when the police pulled in six cars strong.

Once she retrieved her motorcycle, Sarah parked it beside the police building and entered through the front doors. Collins had called her in to say goodbye before she headed up to Maine.

After asking for Collins, she was directed to his office.

She found Detective Munro and Russell already there.

"Everyone's here." She shut the door behind her. "What brings us all together on this lovely afternoon in Vegas?" Her voice still sounded nasally. The bandages wouldn't be coming off her nose for a while yet. Russell looked normal, but she could imagine the size of the bruises under the collared shirt he wore.

"I've discovered something interesting," Collins said. "I thought I'd tell all of you at the same time. Take a seat." Collins directed her toward a chair.

"It's okay. I'll stand." Sarah moved to the side and rested an arm on the file cabinet.

"Sarah, you asked me to look into Russell's history to see what I could find."

She nodded and looked at Russell. He wasn't as nervous as he usually appeared. Something had changed in him.

"I've already talked to Russell about what I found, but I didn't tell him everything."

Russell's head shot up. "What else was there?"

"Well, we know about your daughter, your name change from Michael Mercer, and the family ties to your mother and Sarah's mother." Collins looked at Sarah. She nodded back at him.

She still hadn't called her mother to let her know. She wanted to leave Vegas, endure the open road for a few days to clear her head, and then deal with that phone call. It may cause a larger wedge between Amelia and her sister, but the story needed to come out. She also wanted to see where Russell was going next so they could stay in touch.

"Russell, I understand you're searching for someone yourself," Collins said.

He nodded. "Yes, my real father. My mother claims the

man who raised me was my father, but I've learned that wasn't true. She refused to elaborate, so I left years ago, hoping to find him. Are you going to tell me you've found him?"

Collins walked around his desk and stared out the office window to the street below. "As I searched for all family ties to you, Russell, I did find your father." He turned and looked at Russell.

"But how? There's no public record. I couldn't find anything. It was Penny, or my intuition, that led me to Vegas. I had a feeling that I would find him here. What's his name? Do you know where he lives?" Russell calmed for a moment. "Is he alive?"

Collins nodded. "He's alive. He's very much alive."

"Who is he? Where is he?"

"When I saw the pictures of your mother, I recognized her."

Russell frowned. "What?"

Sarah got it instantly and waited for Russell to catch up.

"I'll be damned," Mara whispered.

"You?" Russell asked.

"Your mother and I spent four wonderful months together here in Vegas. Then one day, she split. No explanation, no call. I found her eight months later and drove up to see how she was doing. She was quite pregnant with you by then. I assumed she had found someone else."

Collins walked around his desk, moving closer to Russell.

"I called your mother yesterday. It took me a while to get her to admit it, but she finally did. She has known about me here in Vegas all these years and never told me about you, my son."

Russell stared wide-eyed at Collins. "That's why Penny got me to send the photos to you. She knew this would happen."

"That's why Vivian brought me here," Sarah added. "It's all connected. It's always connected."

Everyone grew silent for a few moments. The room took on a thickness that could be felt. Sarah breathed in deeply and held it, then exhaled slowly.

Russell moved his butt to the edge of the chair. He grunted and winced in pain as he stood. Russell walked around Collins's desk and stood before him. They stared at each other, then embraced.

The moment brought a tear to Sarah's eyes.

"Nice to meet you, Son," Collins said.

"Nice to meet you, Dad."

Two men at opposite poles, now holding each other as father and son. The one man had feared the law and lived under the shadow of being arrested at any time. The other had kept watch and waited for the right moment to pounce.

They held each other tight and wept.

She was an intruder in their moment. Mara got up and moved toward the door. Sarah joined her.

"Wait," Collins called out. "There's something else."

"Do you want me to tell her?" Mara asked.

Collins shook his head. "No, I have to."

He patted Russell on the shoulder and then walked across the office to stand in front of Sarah.

"There was a man here earlier looking for you."

"What?" Her stomach knotted. She always hated when someone was looking for her. It was shades of Rod Howley and Hank Frommer. "Who was it? Did they identify themselves?"

Collins closed his eyes and nodded. "FBI."

"What did he want?"

"He wants to talk to you, but he gave me a message in case I saw you first."

"What's the message?" she asked and held out her hand.

"He didn't write it down."

She waited, lowering her hand.

"He said to tell you that the Sophia Project has been shut down permanently. He said you would know what that meant."

The Sophia Project was an organization that had hunted Sarah ruthlessly. A psychic research group that had too much power.

"What else did he say?" Sarah asked.

"Just that he wanted to talk to you. Something about a deal."

"A deal?"

Collins nodded.

"You knew I was coming to this meeting. Is he here?"

"No."

She regarded Collins. "Why not? Are you saying you didn't cooperate with a federal agent?"

"That's exactly what I'm saying."

"Why would you do that?"

"Because, Sarah Roberts, you're Russell's cousin. That makes you my family now, too. I protect my family. As far as that agent knows, you're on your way to Vancouver."

It was rare that someone in law enforcement ever did something nice for her other than Parkman.

"Thank you."

"Think nothing of it—"

"He's good," Russell broke in.

They all turned to Russell, who was staring out the office window.

"Who's good?" Collins asked.

"Your FBI agent visitor."

"How is he good?" Sarah asked, already dreading the answer.

"He didn't believe Collins. He decided to wait. I'm hearing that he's inside the building as we speak." Russell turned around. "I'm sorry, Sarah. They mean to take you away. There's something they want you to do for them."

"Can you tell me what it is?"

"All I see is you leaving Vegas in an FBI vehicle if you don't leave this office in less than one minute."

Sarah didn't need any more coaxing. Munro ripped the door open and pushed Sarah out.

"You're going to help me?" Sarah asked.

Munro grabbed her arm and started her along the hall. Collins and Russell followed close behind.

"I know a back way out."

No one said a word as they hit the stairs and ran down to the main floor. At the back door, Munro looked outside. Then she pushed it all the way open and stepped into the blazing sun.

"Your bike's over there."

"Why're you helping me, Munro?" Sarah asked.

"Because you didn't break any laws here. You helped my partner save his brother's life and marriage. Maxwell Ramsey, a known criminal, is off our roster. All you've done is help us. A person like you, Sarah, should not be contained. Go, get out of here. Do what you do best. No one is a better vigilante."

"No one has ever called me that before. I like it."

Collins's phone rang. He answered it, spoke in hushed tones, then ended the call and slipped his phone away.

"That was the FBI at the front counter looking for me. I gotta go."

"Collins?" Sarah said. He looked back at her. "Thanks."

"You don't thank family. It's what we do. Just take care of yourself, and come see me if you ever get back to Vegas. Bring that Parkman guy. I want to meet him."

"Consider it a date. I'll come back one day."

Russell stepped forward. They hugged gently.

"You have to leave," he said. "Now."

Sarah pulled away. "Where will you go?"

"I'm going to stick around here for a few days, get to know my dad better. When my chest heals, I want to go up and see someone in Toronto."

"Toronto? I was just there. Who do you know in Toronto?"

He shrugged. "That's the thing. I don't know. It's what I'm supposed to do. I think a family member is up there."

"Okay, call me sometime."

"Oh, don't worry. I'll be in touch."

Sarah turned to Munro. "Thanks."

"Don't mention it. Now go."

Sarah ran for her bike. She gingerly slipped the helmet over her head, paying close attention to her nose.

Before mounting the bike, she pulled the picture of her sister out of her pocket. When she glanced at the back door of the police station, it was closed. They were back inside.

Wrapped around the picture was a white piece of paper. Sarah unfolded it and read the note. The note Vivian sent her last night. It told her what she had to do and where to go next.

Toronto was her final destination. She smiled to herself. Maybe that was why Russell was heading up there, too. Maine was no longer her destination.

After slipping the note and the picture away, she started her bike and drove out of the police station parking lot en route to the freeway.

Vigilante.

She liked that. What Vivian wanted her to do in Toronto worked well with that title.

Sarah Roberts, *The Vigilante.*

She hit the ramp to the freeway and dipped on the curve until she merged into traffic. Then she opened it up and sped out of Las Vegas.

The FBI car behind her stayed close. She saw it. Vivian told her what to do.

Another chapter was about to unfold for Sarah, and she was ready for it.

When she got to Toronto, she would look up Aaron Stevens. For this next job, she needed to learn how to fight better. Her life hung in the balance. If she picked up anything in Vegas, it was that she needed to learn how to fight like a pro.

Within ten minutes of zigging and zagging, she lost her tail. They zigged when they should have zagged.

Sarah was free.

Free to be a vigilante.

About Jonas Saul

Jonas Saul is the bestselling author of the Sarah Roberts
Series—more than two million sold!—and has written
and published over sixty thrillers. After acquiring an
agent, he signed several deals in Los Angeles, with
MadRiver Pictures optioning his Sarah Roberts Series—
over forty books!—(currently in development).

Jonas has often outranked Stephen King and Dean

Koontz on Amazon over the past decade. He's regularly invited to be a guest speaker, teacher, or workshop presenter at international writing conferences and film festivals worldwide. He hosts an annual writer's retreat in Greece, where he currently lives. He focuses his teaching on how to get tension and emotion in every scene, on every page, how he made it as a creator/writer, the path to success in this business, and the pitfalls to avoid. He also hosts a reading retreat in Greece with guest authors, yoga retreats, and hiking retreats. Visit the Imagine Greece Retreats website at www.imaginegreeceretreats.com, or email him directly to discuss an opportunity to join one of the retreats at jonas@imaginegreeceretreats.com.

Jonas is also a professional freelance editor. He works for several publishers and does private editing for clients, with many testimonials on his website at www.imaginepress.org, which details each author's response to Jonas's editing skills. Email Jonas directly for an editing quote at editor@imaginepress.org.

To book Jonas for a speaking engagement at a writer's conference/festival, to have him on your jury at a film festival, or even to say hello, email Jonas directly at jonassaul@icloud.com.

For updates on releases, hit the "Follow" button on Amazon or Bookbub, and join Jonas on Facebook, where he's most active.

Contact Jonas Saul

Linktree: Find me here

Email: jonassaul@icloud.com

www.ingramcontent.com/pod-product-compliance
Lightning Source LLC
Chambersburg PA
CBHW022124310726

48972CB00007B/2181